j333.95
SIL   Silverstein, Alvin.
            Saving
              endangered animals

HAYNER PUBLIC LIBRARY DISTRICT
ALTON, ILLINOIS

OVERDUES .10 PER DAY. MAXIMUM FINE
COST OF BOOKS. LOST OR DAMAGED BOOKS
ADDITIONAL $5.00 SERVICE CHARGE.

SAVING ENDANGERED ANIMALS

Alvin, Virginia, and Robert Silverstein

ENSLOW PUBLISHERS, INC.
Bloy St. & Ramsey Ave.　　P.O. Box 38
Box 777　　　　　　　　　Aldershot
Hillside, NJ 07205　　　　Hants GU12 6BP
U.S.A.　　　　　　　　　　U.K.

Copyright © 1993 by Alvin, Virginia, & Robert Silverstein

All rights reserved.

No part of this book may be reproduced by any means without the written permission of the publisher.

Library of Congress Cataloging-In-Publication Data
Silverstein, Alvin
Saving endangered animals / Alvin, Virginia and Robert Silverstein.
  p. cm.—(Better earth series)
Includes bibliographical references (p.) and index.
Summary: Discusses the endangerment and extinction of different species of wildlife and conservation efforts now underway.
ISBN 0-89490-402-7
1. Endangered species—Juvenile literature. 2. Wildlife conservation—Juvenile literature. [1. Rare animals. 2. Extinct animals. 3. Wildlife conservation.] I. Silverstein, Virginia B. II. Silverstein, Robert A. III. Title. IV. Series
QL83.S55   1993
333.95'416—dc20   92-1765
                                                CIP
                                                 AC

Printed in the United State of America

10 9 8 7 6 5 4 3 2 1

Illustration Credits: African Wildlife Federation, pp. 20-21; AP/Wide World Photos Inc., pp. 32, 76; C. Kelly, pp. 90, 94; David H. Thompson, International Crane Foundation, pp. 66, 68; Foundation for Field Research, p. 50; Gary S. Harrison, U.S. Fish and Wildlife Service, p. 71; George Gentry, Great Smoky Mountains National Park, p. 52; Great Smoky Mountains National Park, p. 4; Jill Bauermeister, U.S. Department of Agriculture, Forest Service, pp. 15, 81; Lee Emery, U.S. Fish and Wildlife Service, p. 62; Linda Bound, International Wildlife Coalition, p. 110; M. Westervelt, U.S. Fish and Wildlife Service, p. 37; Mark J.Terrill, AP/Wide World Photos Inc., p. 56; Courtesy of Phillips Petroleum Company, p. 103; Rob Stapleton, AP/Wide World Photos Inc., p. 87; Robert A. Silverstein, pp. 31, 96; Rocky Mountain Raptor Program, Colorado State University, p. 92; Ron Singer, U.S. Fish and Wildlife Service, p. 29; Courtesy of Save the Manatee Club, p. 105; Steve Maslowski, U.S. Fish and Wildlife Service, p. 108; World Wildlife Foundation, p. 34.

Cover Photo: Tom Stack & Associates, Thomas Kitchin

Contents

1 Animals in Danger................ 5

2 Society's Role................... 13

3 Saving Animal Habitats........... 25

4 Controversy and Compromises...... 35

5 Back from the Edge of Extinction.... 43

6 Success Stories.................. 59

7 When Disaster Strikes............ 79

8 You Can Help, Too............... 97

   Chapter Notes.................... 111

   Glossary........................ 117

   Where to Write.................. 120

   Adopt-an-Animal Programs......... 123

   Further Reading................. 125

   Index.......................... 127

A red wolf pup at home in the Great Smoky Mountains National Park.

1
Animals in Danger

A traveler was riding down a country road one autumn day when suddenly he heard a great roaring sound. A flock of passenger pigeons swept across the sky, blocking out the sun. Soothing his frightened horse, the traveler rode on. Crowds of men and boys along the nearby riverbank were shooting at the pigeons, but still more birds came. It took three full days for the flock to pass.

The traveler was the great naturalist John James Audubon, and the year was 1813. Audubon calculated that more than a billion birds had passed overhead, and they were only a small portion of the total flock.

Who would have thought that just a century later, in 1914, the last passenger pigeon in the whole world would die in a lonely cage at the Cincinnati Zoological Garden!

Extinct Is Forever

There are many trillions of living creatures, and millions of different kinds of animals and plants share our planet.[1] Each kind, or species, is special and unique. And yet some of these species are in danger of disappearing forever, just as the passenger pigeon did.

When the last member of a species disappears, that species is said to be extinct. Never again will there be another creature of that type on the planet.

Extinction Is Not a New Phenomenon, But . . .

Species have been appearing and disappearing on earth for millions of years. In fact, 99 percent of all the species of plants and animals that ever existed are now extinct![2] So extinction is not something that has just begun happening recently. But there have been some recent changes in the causes of extinction, and there are some worrying signs that species are disappearing much more rapidly now than they did in the past.

Over the past 500 million years, species have become extinct mainly because of changes in the environment or natural catastrophes, such as volcanic eruptions or collisions of meteors with the earth. In the last 300 years, however, thousands of species of plants and animals have become extinct, not because of natural changes but because of the actions of people. Hundreds of thousands of other species may be endangered, too. In fact, according to the

World Wildlife Fund, 20 percent of all the wildlife in the world could disappear within the next twenty years![3]

In the past, extinctions took thousands of years to occur; now they are happening within decades.

Some experts say that species are disappearing at a rate of one a day. But Edward O. Wilson of Harvard University and other biologists have estimated that as many as 17,500 to 50,000 animal and plant species become extinct each year.[4] According to the higher estimate, that's more than 100 living species disappearing forever—*each day!*

Animals become extinct for three main reasons: (1) they are overhunted; (2) they lose their habitats; and (3) pollution makes their habitats unhealthy.

Hunting. People have hunted wild animals for food ever since our early beginnings. Before animals were raised for food, humans had to hunt animals to survive. Some people still rely on hunting for their food. Many others hunt for sport or to sell the animals' furs, hides, tusks, or teeth.

Our planet was once filled with wildlife, and in the past, people hunted without worrying about the future. It seemed there was always more wildlife to be found. But overhunting has caused the extinction of many species. The dodo, a turkey-sized flightless bird that lived on islands in the Indian Ocean, survives today only in old pictures and in the phrase "dumb as a dodo." Sailors found them so easy to kill for food that they soon wiped out every living dodo. The great auk, a penguin-like bird that lived on islands in the North Atlantic Ocean, became extinct in a similar way. Alligators, beavers, koala bears, otters, and whales were saved from extinction through stricter laws protecting them from hunters.

Loss of Habitat. In the past, people thought if you protected animals from hunting, that was enough. But now we know that we must also protect their habitats. This is where they find food, water, shelter, and a place to have their young. Even if they are not hunted, animals will die out if these needs cannot be met.

In this century, loss of habitat has been one of the main causes of extinction. People share the planet with all the

---

Home Sweet Habitat

Many species have developed over millions of years to adapt to a particular environment. A polar bear's thick fur, for example, protects it from the Arctic cold, but it would not survive in a hot desert. Animals' needs may be extremely specific. Koalas, for example, feed on eucalyptus leaves and must live in places where eucalyptus trees grow. Kirtland warblers will nest only in certain areas in Michigan near young jack pines. There are only a few hundred of these birds left, and their fate is very uncertain. They need a large enough area to continue breeding effectively.

Some animals, such as squirrels, raccoons, rats, and sparrows, quickly learn to adapt to a new environment overrun by people. But other animals cannot adapt. If animals cannot find the food they need or cannot adjust to a new and different habitat, they will die out. ■

other creatures that live here. But as the human population grows, people spread out into areas that once were wild, and they compete with animals for living space. Usually the animals lose.

People cut down woods for lumber, clear fields for farms, and fill swamps to build towns, highways, and factories. Land is cleared when we mine for minerals. Wild animals are fenced out so our domestic animals can graze in what were once wild fields. Fences put up in places that used to be wildlands can hinder animals that need large open spaces and make it hard to find food in winter.

When a little piece of land is cleared for a house to be built, the home of a mouse, a groundhog, or a turtle may be destroyed. When a whole city is built in what was once a wild area, an entire species of animals may be endangered. The dusky seaside sparrow, for example, used to be common in the marshes in eastern Florida. But pesticides killed many dusky seaside sparrows, and then the marshes were drained to build highways. In 1987, Orange Band, the last dusky seaside sparrow, died.

People often see wild animals as a nuisance and drive them away into the remaining wildland. But as the world's wildlands disappear, there are fewer places for the world's wildlife to go.

Pollution. Even habitats that are left intact can become unsafe for wildlife because of pollution. Oils spills pollute the oceans and injure and kill water mammals and birds. When farmers spray insecticides to keep insects from eating their crops, some animals may be harmed as well. Factories spew out chemicals into the air, water, and ground. Garbage dumps leak poisonous chemicals into the soil and the water. Garbage dumped into the ocean can poison wildlife; in addition, animals may mistake plastics and styrofoam for food or become strangled by plastic six-pack holders.

Some animals' habitats are poisoned on purpose. Some ranchers, for example, have put out poison for coyotes and wolves because these animals sometimes kill cattle or sheep. They have also poisoned prairie dogs because cattle and horses can be injured when they step into the entrances of prairie dog burrows.

When Extinction Is Most Likely

Animals are in the greatest danger of becoming extinct when they are found in only one place or when their numbers are very small. In such cases the animals in a small area are forced to breed among themselves. Inbreeding increases the chances of inheriting harmful genetic traits. Catastrophes can also wipe out a small population. The heath hen, for example, was once common in the Northeast. By the early 1900s, after years of overhunting, only about a hundred remained. A refuge was set up on Martha's Vineyard, an island off the coast of Massachusetts, and the heath hen population grew. Then, a fire nearly wiped out the population; diseases spread by local poultry farms and killing by cats and dogs added to the losses. By the early 1930s the last heath hens had died.

The Planet Is a Big Ecosystem

Our world is one big ecosystem, and all creatures affect other creatures. If one species becomes extinct, it can change the fate of many others. When wolves and foxes are killed off, for example, the population of rabbits, deer, and other prey animals grows explosively. Then many rabbits and deer die of starvation because there is not enough food for them. When they wander onto people's property looking for food, they are regarded as pests because they eat fruit trees and garden crops.

The Wildlife Debate: Human Needs vs. Wildlife Diversity

Do we humans own our planet, or should we be caretakers of the world, working to preserve it and all of its creatures? This question is being hotly debated these days.

Many people believe that animals have as much right as humans to live on the earth. They believe that the world needs forests and ponds with their many diverse animals and plants and that these things are more beautiful and worthwhile than highways and parking lots.

Others claim the needs of humans come before those of wild animals. Loggers' jobs were pitted against the fate of the spotted owls that live in ancient forests in Oregon, for example. There are no easy answers.

Meanwhile, many people are working to help endangered animals. Local groups rescue injured animals; national and international organizations help stop hunting of endangered animals, fight for stricter laws to protect them, and raise money to save habitats. Refuges and breeding colonies are helping to preserve some of the last members of endangered species, and a start has been made toward re-introducing some of them into their natural homes. Through efforts such as these, some threatened species have made comebacks. But many are still in danger.

2
Society's Role

Until recently, most people believed that the earth and everything on it belonged to humanity and that we could do whatever we wanted with any of the creatures that shared our planet. Not everyone felt that way, though. There have always been some individuals who were concerned about the fate of animals in our world.

In the mid-1700s, for example, a Russian engineer, Peter Jakovlev, was worried about the giant sea cow, which had been discovered in the Northern Pacific Ocean on Copper and Bering islands just a short while before. Jakovlev urged the Siberian authorities to ban the killing of sea cows when hunters visited the islands for hunting expeditions. But no one would listen to him. In a few more years—only about 30 years after they were discovered—the last giant sea cows were killed.

Saved from Extinction

Human activities have driven many species to the verge of extinction, but there have been some encouraging examples of how society can save endangered animals. One of these is the American bison, or buffalo.

The buffalo once was the symbol of the American wilderness. These huge animals roamed the plains, grazing in enormous herds. There were 30 million buffalo in the West in the 1860s. But, by 1883, hunters had killed all but 1,000 of them!

Fortunately, several people had captured some buffalo to raise in captivity. By 1890, 600 of the 700 remaining buffalo were in private hands. Growing numbers of people became concerned that with so few buffalo left, they could soon become extinct.

William Hornaday, the director of the Bronx Zoological Park, which had just been founded, was one of those concerned about the buffalo. In 1891 he convinced zoo officials to set aside twenty acres of the park for a buffalo herd. By 1905 the herd was thriving.

Hornaday and other conservationists wanted to see the American buffalo returned to its natural habitat, so they formed the American Bison Society and convinced Theodore Roosevelt, the president of the United States and an avid outdoorsman, to be its honorary president.

Hornaday and the American Bison Society then set about gaining public support to put small herds of buffalo in various parks, game preserves, and wildlife refuges. The

The buffalo (American bison) was the first big success in the fight to save endangered species.

campaign was publicized widely, and with government support and money raised from the public, buffalo were placed in several areas. By 1934 there were 4,000 buffalo in the United States and 17,000 in Canada, and the species was on its way back from the edge of extinction.

Hornaday's efforts not only saved the buffalo but also made it clear to people in the United States and around the world that many other animals were endangered, too; but people, if they tried, could save them from extinction.

How Society Can Help

There are many ways that people, working through government and other organizations, can help save our wildlife. One is to pass laws that prevent endangered animals from being killed or taken from their natural habitats. Another is to set up parks, refuges, and preserves where the wild habitat is kept intact so that the creatures living on it will remain undisturbed. Today there are more than 400 National Wildlife Refuges in the United States and 3,500 wildlife parks and refuges around the world.

The Endangered Species Act

The Endangered Species Act of 1973 (ESA) was a giant step toward helping endangered animals (defined as animals that are in danger of becoming extinct) as well as threatened animals (those that may become endangered if they are not protected) in the United States and around the world. It established a program that brings together the federal government, the states, conservation groups, individuals, business and industry, and foreign governments in a cooperative effort to save endangered wildlife.

The ESA restricts the killing, collecting, or harming of endangered and threatened animals and makes it illegal to buy or sell, import or export them without special permission. Violators can face a fine of up to $20,000.

The critical habitat of endangered species (the land, water, and air that members of the species need for survival, including places where they live and breed) is also protected under the act. Each year habitats of endangered species are bought up with money from the Land and Water Conservation Fund.

Listing Endangered Species

The endangered and threatened species are listed by the U.S. Fish and Wildlife Service and the National Marine Fisheries Service. Candidates are submitted by anyone concerned about a species of animal or plant, and information has to be gathered to support the claim that the species is endangered.

There are more than 1,117 plant and animal species on the Endangered and Threatened Wildlife and Plants list.[1] Each year about fifty more species are added. More than 4,000 additional species are currently waiting to be added to the list. The case for them may be just as convincing, but limited manpower and funding have kept them from being processed for protected status. Unfortunately, some species cannot wait for all the red tape—according to the Fish and Wildlife Service, 300 species waiting to be put on the list may have become extinct before they could be listed.[2]

Setting Up a Recovery Plan

When the ESA program was set up, the goal was to re-establish endangered species in the wild so they could be removed from the list; but very few creatures have recovered enough for this.

After a species is placed on the endangered or threatened list, the next step is to determine a recovery plan that will help increase the number of animals or plants. Measures include buying more land to preserve their habitats or breeding the species in captivity so they can be released. But setting up effective recovery plans takes a lot of time and money, and only one-third of the species on the list even have recovery plans.

Sometimes it is not easy to find the reason for an animal's decline. And sometimes the reason is found too late—by the time it is discovered, there are very few of the animals left. More than eighty species have been dropped from the list because they were probably extinct already.[3]

Sometimes there are quick solutions. When the insecticide DDT was banned, many species of birds quickly recovered. DDT was making their eggs too brittle to hatch successfully. The brown pelican in the southeastern United

States, for example, was removed from the endangered species list in 1985; removing the harmful pollutant helped it recover. The Arabian oryx and the American beaver recovered when stricter hunting laws were enforced; these animals were being overhunted. The American alligator also made a successful comeback when its endangered status protected it from being hunted and sold as pets. In 1991 federal officials recommended removing a formerly overhunted species, the California gray whale, from the endangered list. This was the first marine endangered species to recover. But John Knauss of the National Oceanic and Atmospheric Administration cautioned that many whales "are still in very bad shape."[4]

Sometimes a species becomes endangered because an animal that was introduced into its habitat is preying on it or competing with it. The greenback cutthroat trout in Colorado was threatened by other fish in Colorado streams. Scientists cleared some streams and re-introduced greenbacks.

Sometimes threatened species can be helped to survive by relocating individual animals. Grizzly bears in Montana, for example, are sometimes captured when they disturb livestock and are moved to other areas where they will not be considered pests.

International Laws

In 1975 an international treaty called CITES (Convention on International Trade in Endangered Species of Wild

Going . . . going . . . gone.

The ivory trade has endangered the survival of the African elephant.

Fauna and Flora) was formed to protect endangered animals from being imported or exported. It has been ratified by more than 100 nations.[5] Every two years they meet to discuss how wildlife is affected by trade. In 1989 the African elephant was added to the list of internationally protected animals to try to stop the trade of ivory that is endangering the elephant. An organization called TRAFFIC monitors the trade of wildlife around the world and alerts authorities when it finds endangered animals are being sold illegally.

Putting Laws into Action

Although laws protecting animals are helpful, they are effective only when dedicated and concerned people make sure that they are used. The battle against extinction is not just a matter of developing a recovery plan to help endangered animals breed and survive better; often it involves a legal battle against developers and other interest groups.

This is the lesson fishery biologist Phil Pister has learned as he and other concerned people fight to save endangered desert fish. Working with the Desert Fishes Council and other environmental groups, they have fought hard to save numerous habitats, such as Devil's Hole near Death Valley, the home of an endangered pupfish. Wells drilled by an agricultural company for irrigation water had lowered the water level in Devil's Hole where the pupfish and other rare species live. Saving this endangered fish by protecting its habitat took a Supreme Court decision limiting the agricultural use of ground water. But then the battle had to be fought on a new front when resort developers began to build roads and divert the water for recreational lakes and golf courses. While environmentalist groups threatened the development with lawsuits, The Nature Conservancy bought more than 12,000 acres of the surrounding wetlands and sold them to the Fish and Wildlife Service. In 1984 these acres, together with other federal lands, became the Ash Meadows National Wildlife Refuge.

3
Saving Animal Habitats

Protecting the habitats of endangered species is often the key to preserving their lives. Many conservation groups such as the National Wildlife Federation, The Nature Conservancy, and the Sierra Club have bought land to protect it in its natural state. (The Nature Conservancy, for example, had purchased more than 3 million acres by the early 1990s.)[1] Federal and state governments are also involved in protecting habitats.

The first national park in the world was Yellowstone National Park, created in 1872. Today national parks and refuges are the home of much of the world's wildlife, and there are wildlife reserves and parks in almost every part of the world.

Wildlife refuges were first set up because people were hunting too many game birds and ducks. President Theodore Roosevelt, who was a hunter, set up the first wildlife refuge in 1903 so that migrating birds would have safe places to stop along their migratory route.

Now, nearly ninety years later, there are more than 400 federal wildlife refuges covering nearly 100 million acres. There are also national parks and forests, state and county parks and reserves, and many private preserves for wildlife in the United States and in other countries.

Islands of Refuge

Parks and reserves often are not perfect, however.

Ecologists have noticed that refuges often become isolated habitat "islands," surrounded by roads, fences, and other man-made barriers. When a large habitat is cut down into a small one, animals that roam large areas (such as bears, wolves, and panthers) disappear. So do the animals that live deep in woods. With less space, there is more competition between animals for food, and predators take a greater toll on populations. Natural disasters such as fires, floods, or disease can completely wipe out a population in a small refuge.

Even the largest refuges may not be big enough. In 1987 ecologist William Newmark reported that fourteen national parks in western North America had lost forty-two species of mammals since they were formed.[2] In the 1980s ecologists such as Larry Harris at the University of Florida pushed the idea of wildlife corridors to connect habitats so that animals could safely pass from one place to another.

The corridor concept caught on, and groups and local governments worked hard to provide safe passageways. Some corridors are only narrow strips, though. For example, a bridge may divert a highway in an area where bears frequently roam. Corridors also allow the passage of undesirable predators, pests, and disease between areas, and they may divert efforts that could have been used to buy whole habitats.

The ideal solution is to make huge corridor areas, such as the 30,000-acre chunk of swampland in northern Florida bought by The Nature Conservancy and the U.S. Forest Service that links two major rivers and allows bears to pass between the Okefenokee National Wildlife Refuge and the Osceola National Forest. According to J. Merrill Lynch, an ecologist with The Nature Conservancy who has helped design huge corridor projects in the southeast, when we focus on animals that need huge habitats, "everything else that requires smaller acreages is going to be protected."[3]

A Worldwide Effort

The number of people in the world increases every day, and more and more of the world's wild areas are being developed. Parks and preserves provide protected habitats for endangered animals, and wildlife in general, all around the world.

Keeping Africa Wild

Many of the world's wild animals live in Central Africa. But Africa is changing as human populations grow. Forests have been cut down, and cattle compete with wild animals for food. Several important wildlife reserves have been set up in Africa to help preserve many wild species.

Return of the Tiger

There are eight different kinds of tigers, and most of them have disappeared from many parts of Asia where they were once quite abundant. Three are already extinct, and most of the others are close to it.

Tigers have always been feared because they attack domestic cows and sheep when hungry and may also attack humans. Some are hunted and killed by villagers to protect their families. Tigers, the largest cats in the world, are also a great prize for sportsmen. Although laws have protected them for many years, poachers still kill them for their valuable furs. Their living places and the wild animals they normally feed on have also been disappearing as forests are cut down.

In the early 1970s Operation Tiger was set up by two international environmental groups, the World Wildlife Fund and the IUCN (International Union of Conservation of Nature), with support from the governments of Bangladesh, India, and Nepal. Through their efforts, nearly a dozen parks and reserves were established, with armed wardens to prevent poaching of the Bengal tiger. The population of deer and wild pigs was also increased to provide enough prey for the tigers so they would not venture beyond the parks in search of food. The program has been fairly successful—by the early 1990s the Bengal tiger population had doubled. ■

International efforts are helping to save the Bengal tiger.

In the late 1950s Bernhard Grzimek and his son Michael did a lot to help protect a very large reserve in Tanzania, the Serengeti National Park. The Grzimeks helped map out the park area, counted the animals that roamed in the 4,500 square miles, and helped plot their migration paths. Local tribes had wanted to make the park smaller, but Grzimek and the books he later wrote helped convince the Tanzanian government about the importance of the reserve. Poachers are still a real problem in Africa, but reserves like this one help protect many wild animals that would have disappeared completely without them.

Save the Rain Forests. Rain forests cover only 2 percent of the earth's surface—but more than half of all the earth's species of plants and animals are found there.[4] According to the National Academy of Sciences, more than 50 million acres of rain forest are being destroyed each year—more than 100 acres each minute!

Rain forests are found in Africa, Asia, and South and Central America. Most of them are being cut down to grow crops or raise cattle. But once a rain forest is cleared, it can only be used for agricultural purposes for a few years. Then the soil becomes unproductive for grazing or growing crops, and new forests are cut down.

Today there are more than 150 groups concerned about the disappearing rain forests. Organizations and governments are working hard to think of solutions to the rain forest problem. Some groups are trying to find solutions that will allow the people to reap benefits by

Gosh, the old neighborhood really has changed!

Quarters contributed by zoo-goers add up to money to preserve rain forests.

preserving rain forests. One is to promote the expansion of markets around the world for products such as Brazil nuts, cashews, rubber, oil, cocoa, and fruits that can be harvested from rain forests without destroying them.

The Nature Conservancy and other groups are also buying areas of rain forests to protect them from development. The conservancy started an Adopt-An-Acre program in 1989 to save Latin American rain forests. By the end of 1991 more than half a million dollars had been raised, and more than one-fourth of it came from young people. Children all around the country send letters of support, and many classes work together to raise money. Justin Leonard, a second-grader in North Carolina, sent a typical letter, "Our class is sending some money to save the rain forest. I like the rain forest. That is why I want to save it. Because if the trees get cut down all the animals will die."[5]

The Nature Conservancy has also provided U.S. zoos and aquariums with modified parking meters decorated with a colorful rain forest scene. When a visitor deposits a quarter, a red-throated hummingbird flies across the jungle scene; the quarters could add up to millions of dollars of donations used to purchase and preserve rain forest land in Costa Rica. San Francisco zookeeper Norman Gershenz thought of the idea, and zoo-goers love it. "It's really neat," remarked Lily Lubin, a nine-year-old visitor to the San Francisco Zoo. "It feels like every time I put a quarter in, I'm saving an animal's life."[6]

Conservation organizations work with local groups in each country to set up a management program to care for the protected rain forests or with local governments to try to establish reserves and refuges. Currently only 5 percent of the tropical forests left in the world are protected as parks or reserves,[7] but in many countries progress is being made.

Some groups focus on replanting trees, which will provide habitats for animals. In Kenya more than 500,000 schoolchildren helped plant 2 million trees.[8] Global Releaf, sponsored by the American Forestry Association, was set up to tackle the problem of deforestation right here in the United States. This program's goal is to plant 100 million trees by 1992.

The Lovable Panda

The panda, with its cuddly, teddy-bear shape, has become the emblem of the World Wildlife Fund and a symbol of the plight of endangered animals. There are less than 1,000 pandas left in the wild, about half of them in the rapidly decreasing wilderness areas in the mountains of western China and the rest in a dozen refuges in China. Another 100 or so are living in captivity in zoos around the world. Matchmaking efforts and the rare captive panda births make headlines round the world. ■

4
Controversy and Compromises

When the Endangered Species Act of 1973 was passed, Congress made an eloquent statement of values, declaring that endangered and threatened species "are of esthetic, ecological, educational, historical, recreational, and scientific value to the Nation and its people."[1]

Not everyone shares those values. Some people think we have already set aside too much land for wildlife refuges. Others point out that only 25 percent of endangered animals in America are protected in national wildlife refuges[2] and fight strongly to protect more.

Everyone Can Win

Activist groups and concerned citizens have halted many development projects around the nation to preserve wildlife habitats. But often the bitterness is just increased on both sides of the political battle, and the victory for wildlife is only temporary. Realistic and workable solutions usually involve some compromises on both sides. When people benefit by allowing a threatened or endangered animal to prosper, both sides win a longer-lasting victory.

Defenders of Wildlife, for example, is using just such a practical approach to help bring the gray wolf back to Yellowstone Park and the Northern Rockies. One of the complaints of the opposition was that wolves might wander into areas where livestock graze. Defenders created the Wolf Compensation Fund, which pays ranchers for any losses that might occur. Compromises like this help make re-introduction programs successful.

Worldwide Efforts

When wildlife species are threatened or wiped out, the whole world loses. People in the United States and many other countries are concerned not only about their own endangered animals but also about those in developing countries in Africa, Asia, and South America. But the most successful animal-saving programs are run by people of the country rather than outsiders. In Africa, for example, groups such as the African Wildlife Foundation (AWF) work with local governments and African people to help conserve protected areas. In addition to funding wildlife programs and supplying equipment such as vehicles, radios, and uniforms to African parks and reserves, the foundation has also set up two African colleges of wildlife

Tourists who come to see African elephants in the wild give local farmers an incentive to protect them from poachers.

management, which have trained hundreds of wardens and rangers who protect African wildlife. The AWF and other groups believe it is very important to make sure local communities take part in managing wildlife so they can feel conservation benefits them, too. Giving people an incentive to save endangered animals can be more effective than strict laws and penalties.

The program to save the addax, an African antelope, is one example. In 1988 there were only fifty addax left.[3] The first step in a recovery plan that was set up by the Nigerian government and the Worldwide Fund for Nature was to establish a national nature reserve. Next, part of the park was set aside as a sanctuary for the antelope—no visitors are allowed to go there without a guide. The town of Iférouane was designated as the gateway to the park. Visitors to the park have to pay a fee and must hire a local guide for tours. The guides enforce the strict park rules,

Developing with Wildlife in Mind

Industry and development are not always pitted against nature and wildlife. Embassy Suites Hotel in Palm Beach, Florida, spent over $200,000 to make sure that their new giant hotel would not harm the sea turtles that come ashore to lay their eggs on a nearby beach. When the hotel was built, special tinted windows were installed to eliminate glare that could disorient the turtle hatchlings, causing them to move toward the dangerous highway instead of the sea. A boardwalk was also built to allow guests to get to the beach without disturbing the turtle nests.[4] ■

including no hunting or cutting of vegetation. The people of the town also benefit from other tourist activities, such as selling crafts and hotel accommodations. This way the animal benefits and the people are also able to make a living, even though they can no longer hunt the addax for food or use the land as they did before it became a reserve.

A similar principle is a key to efforts to save the African elephants. Even before the ivory trade was internationally banned in 1989, many people tried to point out that elephants were much more valuable to Africans as a tourist attraction than for their ivory. About 700,000 tourists visit Kenya each year, for example, and wild elephants are one of the main things they come to see. Farmers in Kenya are paid not to plant crops in elephant ranges so their habitat will be left alone.

The Mountain Gorilla Project offers tours of gorillas in the wild. The money is used to protect the gorillas, and some is given to nearby farmers so local people will view gorillas as an economic resource. Similar programs exist in Nepal to save snow leopards and in Belize, Central America, to save jaguars.

Some people believe that putting wild animals on exhibit creates too much interaction with people, which can cause many problems. The animals on display are no longer living a truly natural life. But for many animals it is their only chance to survive.

Saving Endangered Animals for the Future

Scientists are quick to remind us that endangered animals may be a valuable resource in the future. It is quite common for

Perils of a Sea Mammal

Sea otters have long been hunted for their furs. By the 1890s there were no more sea otters in Mexico, and by the early 1900s none were known to exist off California, either. By 1911 there were only a few colonies of sea otters left in Alaska; in that year, Canada, Japan, Russia, and the United States signed a treaty banning the hunting of sea otters. California also passed a strict bill making it a crime even to own a sea otter fur.

Without the pressure of hunting, sea otters began to make a comeback. In 1938 sea otters were spotted in California for the first time in many years. The small colony grew over the years, and now there are more than 1,000 sea otters off the California coast and close to 50,000 in Alaska.[5]

But the battle was not over. As the numbers of sea otters grew, fishermen began to complain because these animals eat valuable abalone. A heated controversy developed between the fishermen and those trying to protect the sea otters. These sea mammals are also endangered by water pollution, which is becoming more and more serious. A thousand or more sea otters died because of the 1989 oil spill in Alaska. Conservationists are moving sea otters to other locations so oil spills and other catastrophes will not endanger the whole population. They also hope that controlling the number of sea otters in one area will help ease the tension between fishermen and sea otters. ■

people to drive out native animals so their domesticated sheep and cows can graze. But often the decision is short-sighted, as the story of the saiga shows.

By the early 1900s the saiga, a type of antelope in eastern Europe, was nearly extinct. In 1919 the Russian government passed a law making it illegal to hunt the saiga. Scientists suggested that cattle and sheep could not survive in the harsh climate with its scarce vegetation and water.

Rescuing the Rhinoceros

There are only about 11,000 wild rhinos of five living species in Africa and Asia. At the turn of the century, there were more than two million of just one type living in Africa.[6] Poachers armed with machine guns kill rhinos for their horns, which are sold illegally in Asia as a medicinal ingredient.

More and more rhinos are being moved to protected preserves, often with electrified fences and guards who shoot poachers on sight. Recently conservationists have been cutting off the rhinos' horns (under anesthesia) to make them less tempting targets. In the first three years of this program in Namibia, not a single dehorned rhino was killed.

In 1989 a decision was made that should help the black rhinos in Africa. Wildlife conservationists concluded that several subspecies of black rhinos are genetically similar, so they can be interbred. Park rangers will not have to keep the different subspecies apart, and allowing them to interbreed will produce greater genetic diversity. This usually increases a species' ability to overcome diseases and survive in a changing environment. ■

Following the scientists' advice the domestic animals were removed and a saiga breeding program was set up.

By 1970 there were more than two million saiga on the Russian steppes, along with another half-million in eastern Europe, where there had been less than 100 saiga at the turn of the century. Today hunting of the saiga is regulated to keep the population from getting overcrowded. Properly managed wildlife like the saiga can thus provide an important food source, and people benefit by preserving them.

Balancing Conflicting Interests

Pacific salmon draw fishermen to the northwestern United States from all over the world. But hydroelectric power systems and polluted habitats have been killing off huge numbers of salmon. More than 100 stocks are at high risk, and some have already become extinct.

Unlike many other endangered animals, such as the spotted owl, Pacific salmon make a big contribution to the economy. On the other side of the ledger, hydropower greatly reduces the cost of electricity. Groups like Trout Unlimited are working hard to get laws passed to protect the native fish species. They won a major victory in 1991 when the National Marine Fisheries Service recommended listing one species of salmon as endangered and two others as threatened.

5
Back from the Edge of Extinction

When the number of animals of a species gets too low, preventive measures like strict laws against hunting and refuges that keep the habitat intact may not be enough. More drastic measures are needed.

There are many ways to help endangered species recover, ranging from translocation (moving some members of a species from one place to another) to breeding animals in captivity and re-introducing them into their former habitats. Translocation and re-introduction are often a species' last hope for survival, but this is not a permanent solution. The same factors that wiped out the animals' ancestors may still exist and may wipe out the new stock, too.

Translocation

Translocation is sometimes used before the problem becomes so serious that animals have to be removed from their habitat and bred in captivity. Animals are moved from their present habitat to a place where they used to exist but are no longer found, or to a new location. Four species of endangered fish, for example, were moved from one stream in the rain forest in Sri Lanka to another stream system. In four years the new fish population was well established.[1]

Translocation can sometimes be very dangerous, though, and sometimes intentional or unintentional translocations are one of the reasons species are endangered. The brown tree snake, for example, was accidentally introduced into Guam in the 1940s, and it is responsible for the extinction of five different bird species on the island! This is why translocation is used only after a habitat has been carefully studied.

Captive Breeding

When animals can't survive in their habitats anymore, they are sometimes taken out of the wild and bred in zoos, in reserves or refuges, or in special breeding centers. The captive-bred animals may then be released back into the wild to restock a population or to start a new wild population when one no longer exists.

Hi-tech Solutions

Many animals do not breed well in captivity, and special techniques may have to be used. Females may be given hormones to stimulate egg production. Animals or birds may be artificially inseminated. Eggs may be hatched by surrogate parents. Sometimes captive-born birds or animals are raised by surrogate parents in the wild.

In the mid-1980s scientists had success transplanting embryos of endangered animals, which may not breed well, into more common animals. At the Cincinnati Zoo, for example, a rare African bongo antelope was born to an eland antelope, and an Indian desert cat was born to a domestic cat. Zebras have been born to horses, and domesticated cows were used to carry rare African cattle. In each case, the offspring grows up to be like its genetic parents, not like the surrogate mother.

In 1991 a Siberian tiger named Nicole gave birth to a "test-tube baby." Hormones had been used to stimulate and increase egg production in Bengal tiger females. The eggs were removed and were fertilized in a laboratory petri dish (in vitro fertilization). The embryos were placed in Nicole's reproductive tract. Only one of the three cubs born survived, but Mary Alice, the surviving cub, was a major scientific accomplishment—the result of millions of dollars of research. Other animals had been born using in vitro fertilization and artificial insemination, but the Siberian tiger is the biggest animal so far. Researchers at the National Zoo in Washington, D.C., the Henry Doorly Zoo in Omaha, Nebraska, and the

45

Minnesota Zoological Gardens in Minneapolis, Minnesota, collaborated on the project. The team also developed a miniaturized in vitro fertilization lab that can be used in the wild.

The San Diego Zoo and the Cincinnati Zoo have sperm, eggs, and cell tissue from dozens of rare species frozen for future use. The National Zoo is establishing an embryo bank. Some scientists are hopeful that even if a species becomes extinct, techniques that are being developed now could bring the species back. In the future, techniques such as cloning—taking some cells and using the genetic blueprints found in each cell to "grow" an entire animal—could bring back to the world many species that no longer exist.

Animal Dating Service

Zoos and wildlife parks all around the world often work together to help endangered animals. The World Conservation Union's Species Survival Commission has a group of breeding specialists who advise conservationists around the world, providing technical assistance for managing animals in captivity and in the wild.

Working with the American Association of Zoological Parks and Aquariums, zoos cooperate with each other to breed endangered animals. The best matches among animals of different zoos around the world are chosen in a sort of "animal dating service," and zoos loan animals to each other to create breeding programs. Several computer databases list information about specific animals around the world. The Animal Record Keeping System (Arks), which was developed at the Minnesota Zoo, for example, has listings of more than 100,000 animals in 32 countries and is used by more than 300 zoos around the world.[2]

Some databases even include "genetic fingerprints" of the animals. By analyzing the DNA found in most body cells, scientists can figure out an animal's hereditary history. This is actually quite important because many zoo animals in different parts of the world are descendants of the same ancestors that were taken from the wild. Inbreeding can cause health problems. Mating animals with different hereditary backgrounds usually produces healthier, more adaptable offspring.

Teaching Animals to Be Wild

Many problems have to be solved to make it safe for captive-bred animals to go back to their natural homes. Re-introduction requires a lot of preparation. Animals

Zoos: Today's Arks

In the past, zoos just exhibited animals; modern zoos have much more responsibility. They help educate people about the importance of preserving our wildlife and encourage concern for our environment. They also play an important part in saving animals from extinction. Zoo researchers study the reproductive cycles of animals so they can use the information to help the animals reproduce in captivity. Zoos have become major centers for breeding rare and endangered wild animals, and many of the best zoos have large breeding farms. ■

Did You Know . . .

- The California condor is the largest bird in the United States, with a wingspan that reaches nine and one-half feet.

- White rhinos aren't white. Their name is a mistaken translation of the Dutch word *wijde*, which means "wide" and refers to the rhinos' broad, square lips.

- Bald eagles mate for life. They build a nest from branches and twigs and add a new layer to the pile each year. One eagle nest, built in the fork of a hickory tree more than eighty feet above the ground, was used for thirty-five years until it blew down in a storm. It measured eight and one-half feet across and twelve feet deep, and weighed two tons!

- An African elephant eats up to 600 pounds of leaves, branches, bark, fruits, and berries a day. It uses its long trunk as a combination nose, hand, and shower nozzle.

- A newborn baby blue whale is about twenty-five feet long and weights three tons. These whales can grow to 100 feet long, but they feed on two-inch-long shrimp-like krill (a ton of them in one meal).

- The pronghorn antelope is the fastest animal in North America, travelling up to sixty miles per hour. Indians called it the "ghost of the prairie." Refuges set up in the 1920s helped save it from extinction.

- The koala bear of Australia was endangered mainly because of its diet: it feeds only on the leaves of the eucalyptus tree, and settlers cut down eucalyptus forests to make room for farms and towns. Protective laws and island refuges have helped koalas make a comeback.

often have to be taught to be wild so that they can survive in the wilderness. They have to learn how to get food, how to avoid predators, and how to breed and care for their young.

When red wolves were re-introduced into their original habitat in North Carolina in the mid-1980s, for example, they had to be trained how to hunt for food. At first they walked right up to hunters and wandered into populated areas because they were used to people.

In the 1970s and 1980s chimpanzees that were re-introduced in West Africa had to be taught many different things, from how to build a nest, dig with sticks for termites, and avoid poisonous creatures such as scorpions, to how to act properly with other chimpanzees they might meet.

Researchers at the National Zoo in Washington, D.C., found that the captive-bred golden lion tamarins they tried to release in rain forests in Brazil in 1984 could not figure out how to move about in the trees. Instead of swinging on vines and branches as wild tamarins do, they just walked on the ground.

The San Diego Zoo is training lion-tailed macaques to be wild. Eleven of these monkeys live together at the Wild Animal Park. They are being weaned from their zoo food and exposed to predators. When their young are born, they have very little contact with people. In a 1991 *New York Times* article, animal behavior specialist Donald G. Lindburg explained that the project is going well but it would probably take at least five more years of "make-believe"

Before re-introduction into the wild, chimpanzees have to be taught useful skills such as finding food and building a nest. This Liberian chimp is cracking nuts.

wild living before the animals are ready for re-introduction to the mountains of southern India.[4]

Making a Habitat Safe for Re-introduced Animals

Probably the most important factor for a successful re-introduction program is making sure the habitat

Wolves: Wild Again

Wolves were once found all over Asia, Europe, and North America. They can still be found in Asia, but there are very few left in western Europe; in North America they are mostly found in Alaska, Canada, and Minnesota. They have disappeared for the usual reasons: fewer places to live as human settlements spread, hunting for their fur, and extermination by people who regarded them as pests.

The red wolf has been brought back from extinction in the wild by captive breeding programs. In the 1970s, the last forty red wolves were taken out of their wild homes and sent to Point Defiance Zoological Park in Tacoma, Washington. The captive colony thrived, and in 1987 four pairs of red wolves were released in North Carolina's Alligator River Wildlife Refuge. By the end of 1991, four litters had been born at the refuge, making a total of twenty-five wolves there.[3] Wolves were also released on several islands. In the spring of 1991, two pairs arrived at the Great Smoky Mountains National Park in Tennessee. ■

These two red wolf pups were born at St. Vincent National Wildlife Refuge in Florida.

intowhich the animals are being released is protected—and in many cases restored to its original unspoiled condition.

Sometimes endangered animals have to be protected from non-native animals that were introduced into their natural habitat but didn't belong there and now prey on the animal. The Galapagos tortoise and the tuatara, a lizard-like reptile from New Zealand, need to find a home where there are no predators to eat their eggs or compete for food.

Plans also have to be worked out to prevent people from hunting or killing the animals as pests. This is often accomplished by educating communities about endangered species and their habitats. Increasing awareness and concern about endangered species makes it possible to raise more money to fund important re-introduction programs. Moreover, people who appreciate wildlife will take more care to protect endangered animals and their habitats.

After Captive Animals Are Released

When the captive animals are released, the research is not over. Scientists need to know how well the animals survive so they will be able to make new re-introduction programs even better. Often a radio tracking device is used so researchers can follow their progress. The device may be attached to a wolf's collar or a band on a bird's leg, for example.

Saving One Endangered Species Often Saves Many Others, Too

In addition to saving a species from extinction, conservationists have another reason for struggling against the odds to save endangered animals. As long as there are members of an endangered species still alive in an area, their habitat is protected to some extent under the Endangered Species Act.

This is much of the motivation for the massive efforts to save the California condor. The bird's future is quite uncertain, but a lot of effort has gone into trying to save this "ugly" bird in order to keep its habitat protected, too. In 1987 the last California condors were taken out of the wild to be bred in captivity. They would have become extinct if immediate action had not been taken, but this meant that their habitat was no longer legally protected. And yet, as Dr. William D. Toone, curator of ornithology at the Wild Animal Park, explained in a *New York Times* article, "In condor habitat there are 57 threatened or endangered species of plants and animals that nobody cares about. . . . [By] getting people interested in reducing the threats to its survival, many other species will be protected at the same time."[5] Now the scientists had an even greater motivation to restore the California condor to its wild home.

The captive breeding programs at the San Diego Wild Animal Park and the Los Angeles Zoo were even more effective than anticipated. By 1991 there were fifty-two California condors in captivity, and scientists decided to begin their re-introduction program several years ahead of schedule.

In October 1991 two captive-bred chicks from the Los Angeles Zoo, Chocuyens (cha-KEW-ens) and his mate Xewe (GAY-wee), were flown to the Sespe Condor Sanctuary in the Los Padres National Forest, fifty miles from Los Angeles. The birds were taken to a cave where their ancestors had lived. The area around the cave was surrounded by netting. The birds could come and go as they pleased during the day but were shut inside at night. Fitted with radio transmitters so scientists could track them and bring them back if they wandered too far, the experimental pair was set free in January 1992.

Michael Wallace, curator of birds at the Los Angeles Zoo and responsible for the husbandry of half of the California condors in the world today, is "completely confident that we can establish a wild breeding population."[6] If condors can

Condor Breeding Tricks

Biologists learned that if an egg was removed from a condor nest, the condor would lay another egg. Each female's output could be increased to three eggs per year instead of the usual one. The extra condor eggs were hatched in incubators. The chicks were raised in boxes simulating the caves where wild condors live. They were fed using condor-shaped hand puppets so they would identify with their own species when they were old enough to mate. ■

Chocuyens, a captive-raised California condor, takes flight after being released from the Sespe Condor Sanctuary in the Los Padres National Forest.

be re-established in the wild, another major victory for endangered and threatened animals will have been won.

Some Conservationists Are Opposed to Re-introduction Programs

Re-introduction programs are very costly, not always effective, and, at best, just a stopgap measure. Many conservationists think the enormous investment of time and money to try and save individual animals is foolish. What good is it to save a species from extinction if there is no place for them to live? What we should concentrate on, say these environmentalists, is saving habitats and keeping the ecosystem within habitats intact and unspoiled. By saving a habitat, many species of living creatures are preserved.

Some scientists worry that re-introduction programs are giving the public a false sense of hope and accomplishment. If we think that we can simply restock areas that have become low in endangered populations, we can continue to change the habitats the animals need to survive.

They point to "successes" like that of the condor as major compromises. Because condors were endangered due to man-made changes in the environment, scientists are trying to change the habits of the condor to make them able to cope with some of these changes. Using a technique called behavior modification, scientists are trying to teach condors to stay in a certain area and only feed on the carrion that scientists place out for them. This will decrease their chances of dying by flying into power lines, eating carcasses that have been shot with lead bullets, or being shot themselves in unprotected areas.

But some conservationists believe that in retraining wild animals we are making their habitat nothing more than a zoo. They are protected as long as they remain in the managed habitat, but outside it they are no longer safe. A number of scientists believe that in the future there will not be any wild ecosystems left in the world for animals to live in, except for protected nature preserves, zoos, and aquariums.

These are serious reservations to keep in mind as we read about more of the successes of re-introduction programs. Meanwhile, the effort on behalf of endangered species continues, with some groups working to save individual animals and species and others working to save more habitats for them to live in.

6
Success Stories

Have you noticed that nobody is working to save the mosquito or the cockroach? They are in no danger, but some insects are; and there are more species of insects than any other kind of animal. Yet the Xerces Society (named for the first North American butterfly to become extinct as a result of human activities) is the only conservation group focused on insects and other invertebrates.

Justifiably or not, most people care more about the high-profile animals, especially those that are most like us (the mammals) or strike us as beautiful and admirable (such as birds). All too many of these, too, are vanishing, but re-introduction programs have achieved some impressive successes.

Return of the Raptors

Many captive breeding programs have involved endangered birds. There are more than 290 species of raptors (birds of prey), for example, and many of them face uncertain futures. Currently forty-five species of eagles, falcons, hawks, and owls are officially listed as threatened or endangered. With careful study, skilled management, and innovative captive breeding methods, birds of prey can be restored to the wild and once restored can maintain healthy populations.

The success of the peregrine falcon is an encouraging example. Like other birds of prey, this species had been hard hit by the effects of DDT. The insecticide used to be sprayed in many areas to kill insects, but it entered the bodies of birds that ate DDT-contaminated insects or grains, and then was passed on to predators like the peregrine. DDT makes birds' eggs fragile, and they may crack before the young can hatch.

By 1960 there were no peregrine falcons left east of the Mississippi River, and by the early 1970s only 10 percent of the peregrine population in the West remained. Most experts believed the peregrine was doomed.

In 1970 Dr. Tom Cade and a group of graduate students at Cornell University in New York started a research program to learn how to raise falcons in captivity so they could ultimately be released to their former habitat. A large breeding facility, called "the Hawk Barn" or the "Peregrine Palace," was built, and the Peregrine Fund was born.

When DDT was banned in the United States in 1972, the peregrine falcon finally had a chance to survive. With the insecticide danger gone, captive-bred peregrines could be released to breed in the wild. Since the first releases in 1974, more than 3,000 captive-bred peregrines in 28 states have been released by the Peregrine Fund, and other countries, including Canada, Sweden, and Germany, which have similar successful programs. The species is well on its way to complete recovery. Breeding populations have been established in cities (on the rooftops of city skyscrapers, for example) as well as in rural areas.

In 1984 the Peregrine Fund built the World Center for Birds of Prey, the world's largest and most advanced raptor breeding, research, and educational center in the world. Using the captive breeding techniques they developed for peregrine falcons, the center has been involved in breeding twenty-two species, including falcons, hawks, eagles, and owls.

Saving a Symbol

The American bald eagle is also making a comeback from the verge of extinction. In 1782, when the eagle was chosen as our national symbol, there were between 25,000 and 75,000 bald eagles in the lower forty-eight states. By the early 1970s, there were less than 3,000. As for other birds of prey, loss of habitat, pollution, lead poisoning, and illegal hunting had endangered their population.

People have been concerned about the eagle for more than fifty years. The Bald Eagle Protection Act of 1940 made it illegal to disturb or kill bald eagles. A prominent

The bald eagle, our symbol of national pride, is endangered.

figure in the fight to save these birds was Charles L. Broley, a retired banker who became known as "Eagle Man." He banded more than 1,200 birds during the 1940s and 1950s and discovered that eagle reproduction had declined sharply.

The National Wildlife Federation and The Nature Conservancy have bought up eagle habitat, helping stabilize some eagle populations. Captive breeding has brought back bald eagles to areas where they had disappeared.

The first two bald eaglets hatched in captivity were hatched in 1973 at the U.S. Fish and Wildlife Service's Patuxent Wildlife Research Center. This project has grown into the largest colony of captive breeding bald eagles. The eagles are "double-clutched"; eggs are taken out to be incubated, and then the eagles lay more eggs. Three-week-old captive-bred eaglets may be placed in a wild eagle nest to be adopted by new foster parents, or eight-week-old eagles are placed on a tower in a wilderness area and gradually learn to fend for themselves, over a period of weeks. (This gradual weaning into a wild life is called hacking.)

The George Miksch Sutton Avian Research Center near Barlesville, Oklahoma, was the first to double-clutch bald eagles in the wild. Eggs are taken from areas where eagles are plentiful and incubator-hatched; most of the wild eagles go on to lay another clutch of eggs. In 1991, for example, the center was authorized to take seventy-five eagle eggs from nests in Florida as part of a program to establish the eagles in Alabama. "Our goal is to place eagles back in the wild areas where they once flourished," says Steve Sherrod, director of the center. "We'll be running an eagle factory here."[1]

The eggs are transported back to the center in an incubator to be hatched by Cochin hens or (if the shells are too thin) in an incubator. The center is careful to make sure the eagles don't imprint on humans (that is, identify with their human caretakers instead of their own species) by using special one-way windows and eagle-shaped hand puppets to feed the eaglets. The program has been very successful. (A cracked egg glued on the site with Super Glue even produced a healthy eagle.)

By the early 1990s there were more than 5,000 bald eagles, and over a dozen states are working on programs to re-introduce eagles into the wild.

Long-range Effort

Seven of the fifteen species of cranes are currently endangered, and the whooping crane is one of the rarest birds in the world. Scientists did not believe this bird had a chance to survive. In 1941 there were only sixteen whooping cranes in Texas where they spent their summers. Not much was known about them—it was not even known where they went to nest and hatch their eggs. In the mid-1950s a pilot returning from fighting a forest fire spotted a whooping crane family at the Wood Buffalo Park in Canada, thousands of miles away.

This tall bird, with its stilt-like legs and distinctive whooping cry, caught the public's fancy. Each year people all over the country eagerly awaited the results of the latest whooper census. As concern grew, recovery programs were set up. The Texas winter feeding ground was turned into the Arkansas National Refuge to protect the whooping crane. Cooperative efforts between Canada and the United States have helped protect the whooping crane over much of its migratory route. The remaining wild flock gradually increased, to nearly 140 as of 1991.

A program to breed whooping cranes in captivity was set up in 1967, just in case something happened to the wild flock. Whooping cranes typically lay two eggs at a time, but usually only one of the hatchlings survives. Scientists removed the extra egg from whooping crane nests and hatched them at the Patuxent Wildlife Research Center in Laurel, Maryland. The twelve hatchlings were the start of a captive flock.

Various techniques increase the effectiveness of captive breeding. The twenty-two hours of daylight that the wild birds experience in northern Canada during the nesting season is simulated with floodlights. Artificial insemination increases the number of eggs laid. Eggs are removed from the nest to be hatched in an incubator or by a sandhill crane surrogate parent; meanwhile, the whooping crane may lay more eggs. Imprinting is avoided by feeding the chicks with whooping crane hand puppets.

Wearing a crane hand puppet, a volunteer at the International Crane Foundation keeps two whooping crane chicks from fighting.

By 1989 there were fifty-three captive-bred whooping cranes at Patuxent. The Fish and Wildlife Service decided to split the captive-bred flock to reduce the chance that disease or natural disaster might wipe out the entire captive population. Late in 1989, half the flock was flown to Baraboo, Wisconsin, where the International Crane Foundation (ICF) has successfully bred fourteen of the world's crane species. The ICF was founded in 1973 by Ron Sauey and George Archibald, who were worried about the cranes. Their program has helped cranes on five continents, and they have developed captive breeding techniques used for many bird species.

One of the goals of whooping crane captive breeding programs is to establish additional wild flocks in case something happens to the one in Texas. The numbers are still so small that a major oil spill, disease, or some other disaster could wipe out the entire wild population.

Dancing with Whooping Cranes

George Archibald, the director of the International Crane Foundation, made the news when he successfully got a whooping crane named Tex to lay eggs by dancing the cranes' courtship dance with her. (Tex was imprinted on humans and refused to mate with male whooping cranes, but she was very fond of Archibald.) The eggs were fertilized by artificial insemination, and the first chick to hatch was named Gee Whiz. Since then, Archibald has taken part in several successful mating dance rituals with other species of cranes as well.[2] ■

Dr. George Archibald dances with the captive-bred whooping crane "Gee Whiz." This mating dance will prepare her to lay fertile eggs.

In 1975 a program was set up, placing whooping crane eggs in sandhill crane nests. The sandhill cranes have a much shorter and safer migratory route. Researchers hoped that the whooper chicks would adopt the migration pattern of their foster parents and establish a new wild flock with a better chance for survival. The new flock, which summers in Idaho, now includes thirteen whooping cranes. But none of them have mated!

In late November 1991, ICF sent a whooping crane chick named Wisconsin, hatched in Baraboo, to the U.S. Fish and Wildlife Services' Patuxent Wildlife Research Center to join four other chicks. The five chicks were scheduled to be released at Kissimmee Prairie in central Florida in early 1992. They will be monitored with radio transmitters. If they are successful, more chicks will be released to establish a new wild flock.

Fish Story

More then 350 fish species in North America are threatened, and more than ninety are endangered. One of the most important reasons is that as human developments expand, water systems are being polluted and even disappearing. Sometimes introducing new species has endangered the native fish of the area. The Gila topminnow, for example, used to be one of the most abundant fish in southern Arizona. But then the mosquito fish was introduced to control mosquitoes and competed with the topminnow. The disappearance of the shallow-water habitats where the minnow lived added to the threat, but now the fish is making a comeback. Captive-bred minnows were introduced into nearly 200 different sites. The Gila topminnow is now out of immediate danger, but it remains to be seen whether the same conditions that caused it to be endangered will develop again.

Turtle Tales

Reptiles have also been bred successfully in captivity. The most endangered of all the sea turtles, the Kemp's ridley sea turtle, was once very abundant in the Gulf of Mexico: There were more than 30,000 nesting females there in the 1940s. By the 1970s there were only a few hundred left. All six of the giant sea turtles found in United States waters are either endangered or threatened animals and so are protected under the Endangered Species Act. Many other governments have banned or limited the killing of sea turtles. But the giant sea turtles are still endangered for several reasons.

Although they live in the ocean, female sea turtles travel great distances to return to the beach where they were born to lay their eggs. If people disturb the nests, the eggs can be damaged. Many giant sea turtles are killed in huge nets used to catch shrimp. The turtles become entangled in the nets and drown because they can't get to the surface for air. Pollution, such as oil slicks, can also harm sea turtles. Floating plastic looks like a jellyfish to turtles, and they can choke when they gobble it down.

Green sea turtles like this one travel great distances through the ocean to lay their eggs on the beaches where they were born.

To solve some of these problems, fences are often put up on beach nesting sites to keep people away. And late in 1989 the Department of Commerce ordered all shrimp nets to use Turtle Excluder Devices—trapdoors that let turtles escape.

A "head start" program is helping save sea turtles. Eggs are gathered from the beaches and are incubated and hatched in captivity. The turtles are then brought back to the beach for imprinting, so they will later know where to come back to lay their eggs. The turtles are released when they are big enough to be safe from most predators, and they are tagged so scientists can study their behavior.

A type of tortoise called the angonoka is one of the most endangered reptiles in the world. African bush pigs that were introduced into its habitat in northwestern Madagascar prey on angonoka eggs and young. More than ten hatchlings have been produced in captivity at the Ampijoroa Forestry Station at Madagascar. When these are old enough, they will be used to restock the endangered reptile.

The tuatara on New Zealand is another reptile that may be saved from extinction by captive breeding programs. Victoria University researchers are now working with one species that was down to a colony of only 300 on one small island. Wild females are given hormones to stimulate egg-laying, and the eggs are hatched in incubators.

Re-introducing Rare Mammals

There have been relatively few attempts to re-introduce endangered mammalian species so far, mainly because of the high costs, difficulties, and shortage of suitable habitats. But during the 1980s, there was a surge of new programs, working with rare mammals such as the brush-tailed bettong (a marsupial), the red squirrel, swift fox, Arabian oryx, and the chimpanzee.

Successful re-introduction requires a careful selection both of the animals for the program and of their potential habitat. The animals may have to be taught how to survive on their own. In the Gambia project in Senegal, beginning in 1973 researchers lived full-time with chimpanzees, teaching them how to build nests, avoid getting stung by scorpions, use a rock to open baobab pods, fish for termites with twigs, and get along with other chimpanzees. After the animals are on their own, radio tracking devices and

Saving the Unicorn

Scientists believe that the Arabian oryx, with its single horn, was the basis for the unicorn legend. But in this century, it looked as though this real-life antelope would soon vanish like the mythical beast. In 1961 there were only nine oryx left in the world! Breeding programs, such as the one at the San Diego Wild Animal Park, have been very successful. Today there are hundreds of Arabian oryxes, and herds have been re-established in protected wild areas in the Middle East. ■

other means are used to monitor their success—while at the same time trying to avoid too much contact with humans.

Freeing the Ferret

The black-footed ferret is the only species of ferret found naturally in North America and is considered one of the rarest mammals in the world. It was thought to be extinct, but in 1981 a group was found in Wyoming. These animals were nearly wiped out in the mid-1980s by disease. In 1986 the Wyoming Game and Fish Department captured the remaining wild ferrets to be bred in captivity.

Leave It to Beavers

Beavers are an important part of an area's ecology. The dams they build along rivers help keep valuable topsoil from being washed away. But beavers were once killed by the millions for their soft, thick fur. By 1900 there were very few beavers left in North America.

As people became more concerned about endangered animals, many states began setting up re-population programs to return beavers to the woods and meadows where they had once lived. In Montana beavers were placed in wooden boxes and dropped into remote wilderness areas with special parachutes. When the box landed, the door sprung open and the animal was free. In Maine, guides backpacked beaver boxes into wilderness areas to set them free. Alabama had only 500 beavers at one time. In a few years there were 200,000. Beavers are no longer endangered. ■

They thrived, and by late 1990 there were nearly 120 in the colony.

Many innovative techniques were used to help the program succeed. Siberian polecats, a closely related species, were used as surrogate mothers to raise the ferret kits. Young ferrets were chased with a stuffed owl and Robo-Badger (the head and front paws of a stuffed badger mounted on a remote-controlled toy truck) to teach them to avoid predators. They were taught to hunt their main food source, prairie dogs, in special areas with prairie dog colonies.

The ferret project is being financed by the U.S. Fish and Wildlife Service and the Wyoming Game and Fish

A Whole Ecosystem

Ferret re-introduction presented the problem of finding a suitable habitat with enough prairie dogs to support a ferret population. From an estimated 6 billion in the time of the pioneers, prairie dog numbers had been greatly reduced by private and government-sponsored extermination programs. (Ranchers and farmers considered these rodents pests because cows and horses could stumble in prairie dog burrows and break their legs.)

Biologist Brian Miller and others involved in the ferret recovery program believe that prairie dog poisoning should be stopped. "One of the main things that's wrong with endangered species programs is there's too much single species management," Miller says. "With the black-footed ferret especially, there's a chance to save an entire ecosystem instead of concentrating on one animal."[3]

This healthy litter of European ferrets, born in 1987, was the first ever produced by artificial insemination. Researchers at the National Zoo in Washington, D.C. bred them to develop techniques for saving the black-footed ferret from extiction.

department. They hope to start ten colonies of ferrets and to establish 1,500 ferrets in the wild, which would take them off the endangered list.

The first two ferrets were released with collars for biologists to track their progress at a festive ceremony in September 1991, when Wyoming governor Mike Sullivan told the ferrets to "go forth and multiply."[4] Additional programs are being set up to establish ferret colonies at zoos in Virginia and Nebraska.

7
When Disaster Strikes

Saving animal species is an important goal for many concerned people. But sometimes individual animals are endangered, too. Disasters like hurricanes, or more often man-made disasters such as oil spills, can kill large numbers of individual animals in an area. When catastrophes happen, volunteers usually leap into action all around the world.

Alaska

In 1989 the entire world was shocked when the tanker *Exxon Valdez* struck a reef in Prince William Sound in Alaska and 11 million gallons of oil leaked into the water, fouling 1,200 miles of shoreline. Before the spill this had been one of the cleanest, most untouched areas in the world.

Many animals were endangered by the oil, but sea otters were most affected by the disaster. Oil makes their fur clump together, which makes it no longer waterproof. The animals can then freeze to death from the cold water. It is estimated that between 1,000 and 3,000 sea otters died, as well as nearly 40,000 birds.[1] In addition, many larger mammals have eaten contaminated food, which could affect their reproduction and survival in the future. Scientists are also worried because contamination can affect humans through the food fish such as salmon and herring caught in the once pristine waters.

After the accident, three rescue centers were set up. For months thousands of volunteers and experts from all over the world worked to clean up the area and save birds and otters.

Veterinarians from across the nation were flown to Alaska to help coordinate the rescue efforts. Dr. Judith McBain was one of the vets who flew to Valdez for two months to head one of the rescue centers. She and a team of volunteers worked hard to save sea otters and seabirds. A team of four people worked together washing and rinsing each otter for several hours. Each animal was tagged and carefully monitored by veterinarians. After they were cleaned, they were blown dry and fluffed with hot-air hoses.

Many otters appeared to be suffering from internal problems because they had tried to lick off the oil to clean themselves, so Dr. McBain sent six sick otters to her

Volunteers work to clean off a sea otter covered with oil.

veterinarian husband at Sea World in San Diego, California, where the otters were given various tests. Working over the phone the doctors developed a treatment program for the poisoned otters.

A total of 357 otters were brought into the centers, and about 200 were saved and returned to unpolluted nearby waters.[2] Orphaned babies and others were sent to aquariums. Dr. McBain and six other vets received awards for their efforts.

After the *Exxon Valdez* oil spill, Congress created a $1 billion cleanup and liability fund, which is financed by a tax on oil.

California

In 1988 365,000 gallons of oil leaked into San Francisco Bay from a faulty pipe. The oil spread rapidly into waterways and marshlands, killing and injuring hundreds of animals and birds.

Rescuers sprang into action trying to save oil-soaked birds and mammals. Volunteers were led by two experienced wildlife rehabilitators, Esperance Anderson and Alice Berkner. Both had first become involved with rescuing oil-soaked animals in 1971 when they volunteered to help after two tankers collided under the Golden Gate Bridge and 7,000 birds were endangered. After their volunteer work in 1971, they both continued in careers helping distressed animals. Esperance Anderson became the co-head of the "Oiled Bird Team" at the Lindsay

Museum in Walnut Creek, California, which educates young people about the environment and offers a wildlife rehabilitation program. Alice Berkner helped found the International Bird Rescue Research Center in Berkeley, California. The two women and many volunteers worked up to thirteen-hour days in the weeks after the 1988 San Francisco spill, washing more than 400 birds and animals.[3]

Washington

In December 1988 as many as 40,000 birds died when 230,000 gallons of oil leaked from an oil barge off the southern coast of Washington, coating beaches from Oregon to British Columbia.[4] Thousands of birds were coated with oil so their feathers no longer provided insulation against the cold water, and many could not float or fly.

The Washington State Department of Ecology quickly began to coordinate a rescue plan. An emergency rehabilitation center was set up at a local school, and volunteers constructed pens for the birds while other volunteers (including several high school classes) combed the beaches for oiled birds. At the school, birds were fed three or four times a day using rubber tubes attached to syringes.

Meanwhile, cleaning facilities were being set up at another location, and a few days later the birds were moved one by one in cardboard boxes. There volunteers worked in teams to wash the birds—one person held the bird and another washed it in buckets of soapy water. The birds were scrubbed with toothbrushes, and then they were rinsed to get out all the soap. It took nearly an hour to clean each bird.

The rescue effort was supervised by Ron Holcomb of the Department of Ecology, Don Kane of the U.S. Fish and Wildlife Service, and Alice Berkner, executive director of the International Bird Rescue Research Center. More than 9,000 birds were brought to the center. Two-thirds had died before they even arrived, and 2,000 could not be saved. Nearly 1,000 birds were rescued and released by the time the center closed a month later. Don Kane was proud of the work the volunteers did. "Two thousand caring men and women donated tens of thousands of hours . . . in an effort to rescue these birds . . . it was an effective response."[5]

Animals along the Washington coastline had not fully recovered from the damaging effects of that oil spill when another oil spill occurred in July 1991 off Washington's northwest tip. Thousands of birds and mammals along the shores of Olympic National Park were endangered. The area was home to many different animals, including more 100,000 sea birds, as well as sea otters, sea lions, seals, and whales. Washington State Department of Wildlife spokesman Doug Zimmer pointed out that even birds like eagles and peregrine falcons were also threatened because they tried to feed on the carcasses of oil-soaked birds, which would affect their long-term health and ability to reproduce.[6]

Temporary centers were set up to feed and clean the birds and sea otters. The animals were taken from the contaminated beaches in cages and sent to a center in St. Edwards State Park, in a former seminary, where volunteers worked to clean and feed the oil-soaked birds while plumbers and carpenters worked to set up other facilities.

Makah tribal member Bobby Rose was one of the volunteers in charge of getting oil-soaked birds to the cleaning facility. A licensed bird rehabilitator, she had also helped with the rescue two years earlier. A month after the 1991 spill, 800 birds had been treated and cleaned. Bobby Rose brought seven of the rescued birds back to Neah Bay where many oiled birds had been found so they could be released while local children watched. Many of the children, such as eleven-year-olds Deanna Buzzell and Ida Colfax, had worked hard as volunteer bird cleaners. Bobby Rose had requested the opportunity to release some rescued birds as an uplifting experience for the young volunteers. "I thought that since some of the kids here have worked two oil spills and all they saw was dead and oiled birds that it would be nice if they could see the complete circle with live ones going back."[7]

Argentina

In September 1991, students from a nearby university rushed to the rescue of penguins that were climbing onto a shore in Argentina coated with oil. At least 16,000 penguins died from what appears to have been an unreported oil spill off the Argentine coast. A month before, wildlife in the area had been hit with another disaster—a volcano erupted, spewing out ash and devastating the environment.

The Persian Gulf

War is always a horrible thing, but the war in the Persian Gulf was particularly devastating to the environment and to animals in the wild. The Arabian peninsula is a major migratory route as birds travel from Africa to breeding grounds in Asia. The Persian Gulf is rich with plant and animal life, so it is a common place for migrating birds to stop. Oil poured into the Gulf due to Iraq's actions and resulted in the world's largest oil slick, endangering countless birds, mammals, and wildlife habitats.

Unlike other clean-up attempts after oil spills, volunteers had to work under wartime conditions. The Saudi government set up a bird-cleaning center. Nurses and military personnel who had originally come to help human casualties, as well as ordinary soldiers waiting to be shipped home and Saudi citizens, volunteered to help clean the birds at the center. Several hundred were saved, but at least 20,000 birds died.

Green turtles and endangered hawksbill turtles crawl ashore on several islands off the Saudi coast to lay their eggs. Experts were concerned because the turtles would be coming soon, but the islands were covered with oil and debris. British and American marines cleaned up four of the islands just in time. The very day they finished, an early hawksbill turtle wandered onto one of the islands.[8]

After the oil tanker Exxon Valdez ran aground in Prince William Sound, volunteers from all over the world went to Alaska to help save the injured wildlife. These volunteers are cleaning an oil-soaked cormorant.

Animals at the Kuwait Zoo were also affected by the war. Iraqi soldiers killed many of the prized animals and stole many others to be taken to Iraq. Some animals were saved, however, because of the bravery of neighborhood residents. Every day they sneaked past Iraqi soldiers on guard to give food and water to the animals left in the zoo.

Puerto Rico

Today scientists use computers to figure out how best to protect endangered animals. A computer study of Puerto Rican parrots concluded that these birds were most threatened by disease and natural disasters such as hurricanes. Precautions were taken to lessen the effects of a major catastrophe. After Hurricane Hugo hit Puerto Rico in 1989, there were only thirty parrots left in the wild. Half the parrot population was killed in the hurricane, but many more would have been lost if the scientists' advice had not been taken.[9]

Massachusetts

Scientists are not sure why whales become stranded on beaches, but in recent years it has become much more common. Whenever whales become stranded on Massachusetts beaches, members of the New England Aquarium staff can usually be found supervising the rescue attempts. Whales are also sometimes brought to the aquarium facilities in Boston, where they are rehabilitated and later released.

What Should You Do If You Find an Injured or Abandoned Wild Animal?

In a free booklet, *You Can Do It*, the National Wildlife Federation has some good advice about what to do if you find an injured or orphaned wild animal. You should not try to help an injured wild animal yourself. An injured animal may bite or scratch because it is scared. It may be carrying a disease, such as rabies, that can make you sick. It is also illegal to keep many wild animals as pets without special permission.

If you find an injured wild animal or bird, leave it where it is and call your local animal shelter, nature center, or game warden for help. They may be able to help you locate a licensed wildlife rehabilitator who can take care of the injured creature.

If you find a wild animal that seems to have been deserted by its family, don't touch it—its mother may just be away getting food. If it is still by itself a few hours later, call for help just as you would if it were injured.

Wildlife Rehabilitators

Across the nation there are countless groups and individuals who provide for the rescue, medical care, rehabilitation, and release of injured or disabled wild birds and animals. Many are licensed individuals working from their homes or veterinarians who donate their time and services. There are also extensive volunteer networks, such as Volunteers

Squirrels at the Stonehedge Conservatory in New Jersey find a cozy hangout in an old sock.

for Wildlife on Long Island, New York, which has a network of eighty veterinarians who treat injured wildlife without charge. Since 1981 they have responded to nearly 50,000 calls for assistance.

Rehabilitation centers like the Wild Animal Clinic in Monroe, Washington, can tell many heartwarming tales of injured wildlife that are nurtured back to health and ultimately released. Their guests have included Goldie, a two-week-old fawn that was injured by a car; Ninja, a turtle whose cracked shell was repaired with fiberglass resin; Kermie, a bullfrog with an injured leg; and Rainbow, an osprey (bird of prey) that needed a little help during its long migration from Mexico.

Wildlife rehabilitators enjoy the thrill of being able to help injured wild animals recover and ultimately be returned to the wild. But most of them are nonprofit organizations that need financial help from the public. Many are also grateful for any volunteers who can offer their services, too.

Rocky Mountain Raptor Program, Colorado. The Rocky Mountain Raptor Program (RMRP) was started in 1979 when some veterinary students at the Veterinary Teaching Hospital at Colorado State University helped care for injured birds of prey. In the early 1980s they received a grant to buy a small building and holding pens for the birds. The group was run as a student club with a faculty advisor. In 1987 with the aid of another grant they hired a director, Judy Scherpelz, to recruit volunteers from the

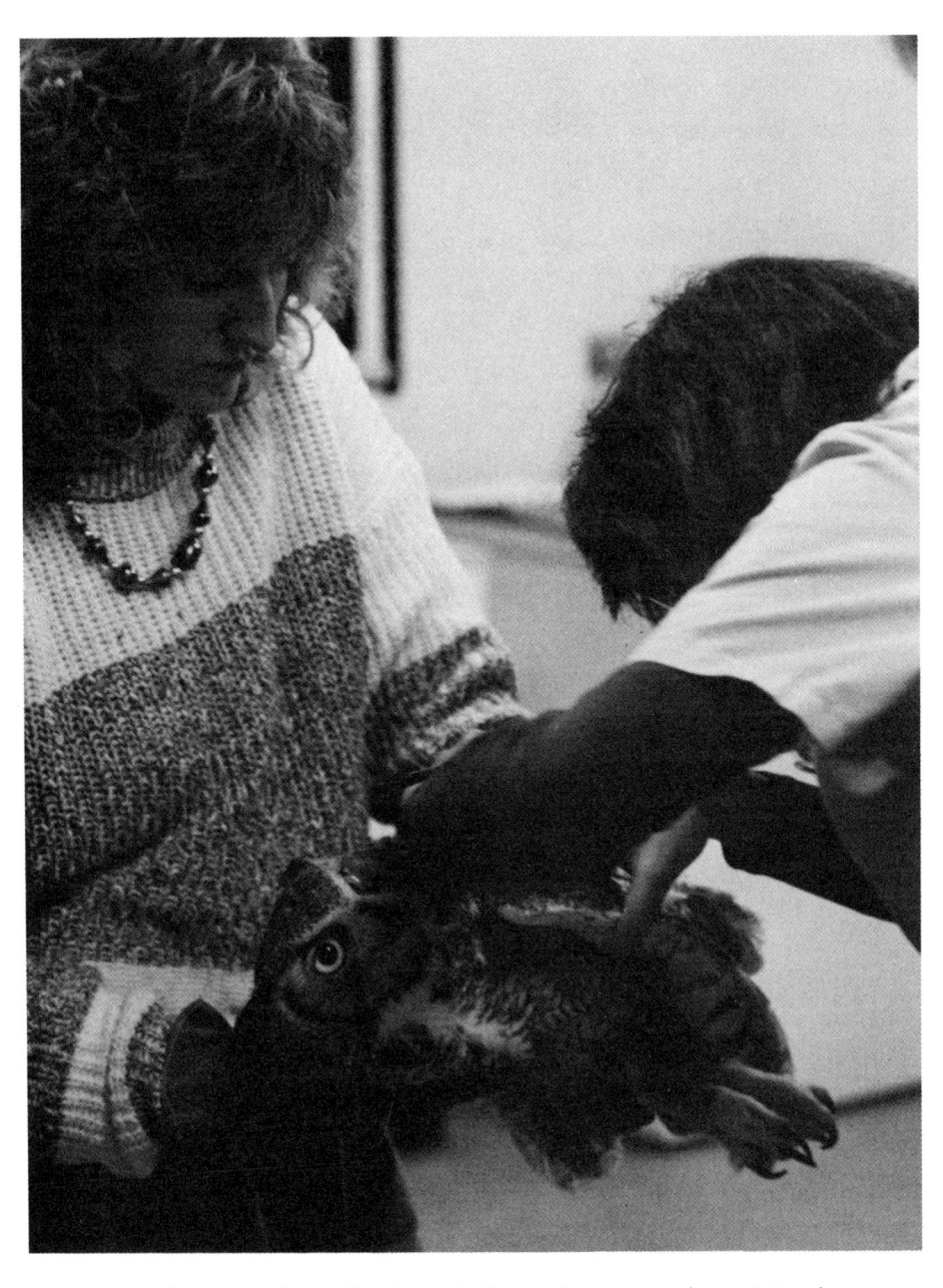

Volunteers at the Rocky Mountain Raptor Program tend to an injured Great Horned Owl.

community, to raise all operating funds, and to develop a community education program. Four years later the RMRP was treating more than 125 birds each year, had more than 100 volunteers, and was giving about 135 educational presentations to more than 10,000 school children in Colorado each year.

Most of the injured birds are released after they are treated, but those that are not able to survive in the wild are used in the educational presentations. Judy Scherpelz and volunteers bring raptors like eagles, falcons, hawks, and owls to elementary schools to teach children the importance of birds of prey. "One way to improve the world is to educate our young people so that they will eventually make lasting contributions to our environment," she says, "and in addition to helping individual injured birds, that is their goal."

Stonehedge Conservatory, New Jersey. For Charlene Kelly, taking care of birds grew from a backyard hobby to becoming a licensed bird rehabilitator. After being an avid bird-watcher for years, she began to band birds in her backyard. Local children called her the "Bird Lady" because of her interest in birds and began to bring her injured birds that they had found. She started a banding and rehabilitation center in her backyard and took care of many injured birds, including endangered species such as a bobolink. After an article about her efforts appeared in a local paper, she received many donations and letters of support.[10]

A Stonehedge Conservatory volunteer demonstrates the incorrect way to feed baby birds. To avoid imprinting, they should not be allowed to perch on people's fingers, shoulders, or heads.

The article told about a male Eastern bluebird that she had helped. Cherpy was healthy, but when he was brought to the center he was imprinted on humans and too tame to be let out into the wild. Charlene Kelly tried unsuccessfully to make Cherpy wild again by placing him with an oriole for a while. After the article appeared, Cherpy was introduced to a female bluebird that had been rehabilitated. Cherpy quickly lost interest in humans, and instinct took over. After several weeks the two bluebirds were ready to be released into the wild.

Meanwhile, a friend offered the use of his stables as a breeding station for rare, threatened, and endangered species. Shortly afterward, someone who had read the local article donated thirty acres of wetland to her group, the Stonehedge Conservatory. A caring woman and a story about a bluebird have helped not only many injured birds but many other animals that live on the now-protected land.

I WANT YOU
To Help Save Endangered Animals!

8
You Can Help, Too

A herd of rare English pigs was headed for the slaughterhouse when the owner could not get a bank loan for his breeding farm. But when the London *Daily Telegraph* publicized the story, British animal lovers sent nearly $5,000 in donations. Prince Charles added a personal contribution to fund a classroom on the farm, where children can learn about animal husbandry. Meanwhile, former Beatle Paul McCartney and his wife Linda bought eighty acres of woodland in southwest England for a deer sanctuary.

In addition to celebrity newsmakers, many highly trained people in the world are trying to help save endangered animals and the environment they live in. But there are even more ordinary people helping out. In fact, there are many things you can do, too.

Hints for Helping Wildlife from the National Wildlife Federation (NWF)[1]

1. Build and take care of bird feeders (NWF offers a booklet on how to recycle containers into bird feeders, *Recycle for the Birds.*)

2. Provide water for wildlife. (Learn how to build a drip pool in *Ranger Rick* magazine, September 1988, page 47.)

3. Build nesting boxes for birds. (Plans to build bluebird and barn owl boxes are available.)

4. Provide nesting materials for birds. (In the spring, hang an onion bag filled with yarn, string, dryer lint, or hair.)

5. Plant a "butterfly garden." (The April 1987 issue of *Ranger Rick,* page 31, has a list of plants that butterflies like.)

6. Make houses for bats. (Plans for a bat box are available for $1 from Bat Conservation International, c/o Pat Morton, P.O. Box 162603, Austin, TX 78716.)

7. Build a rock pile for small mammals and reptiles to hide in.

8. Brush piles make great hiding places for birds and small animals.

9. Turn your yard into a "Backyard Wildlife Habitat." (A free NWF brochure offers suggestions and tells you how to get your yard certified as an official Backyard Wildlife Habitat.)

The Zoological Society of San Diego adds an important caution: Leave animals in the wild. Turtles, lizards, butterflies, and crabs are fun to watch, but don't take them out of their habitats.[2]

More Suggestions for Helping Wild Animals from the Defenders of Wildlife[3]

1. Don't buy items made from endangered or threatened species.

2. Don't buy exotic wildlife such as wild-caught birds, for pets.

3. Don't use chemicals on your lawn or garden. They kill birds, small mammals, and insects that are helpful to humans.

4. Reduce, reuse, recycle, recover! (If we don't use energy wisely, we have to destroy more wildlife habitats to find oil, coal, or water to build dams for energy.)

Studying Wildlife from Your Window

The BirdBox program, offered by the Phillips Petroleum Company and the Oklahoma Department of Wildlife Conservation, helps young people experience wildlife. Schools can purchase easy-to-assemble nesting boxes for birds (30 for $35), and students can watch and study the habits of birds that live in their area. ■

5. Join a wildlife protection club. If there isn't one in your school or neighborhood, start one.

6. Sponsor a cleanup day where you live. Plastic rings, fishing lines, and glass are some of the items that trap and injure wildlife.

7. Write to your local, state, and federal officials, asking them to protect wildlife. They will listen if you get other students to write lots of letters about a problem in your community or state.

Kids Can Make a Difference

Andrew Holleman, a Massachusetts seventh-grader, won an award from the Environmental Protection Agency (EPA) for helping save a wildlife habitat near his home. He had read in the paper that a developer was planning to build condominiums in an area where there were woods, fields, and swamps.

Exotic Animals Don't Make Good Pets

Cats, dogs, and some other animal species have been domesticated for so long that they really need to be with people. But many people think it is cruel to try to turn wild animals into pets. Moreover, the pet trade is helping endanger wildlife. From 8 to 20 million birds are captured and taken as pets each year, for example.[4] Many birds die or become sick while being shipped around the world—as many as half don't survive the trip. More than 10 percent of the bird species in the world are threatened with extinction, including seventy-seven types of parrots. ∎

Andrew was worried that the development would take away the homes of all the animals that lived in the area.

Andrew contacted a local Audubon group for ideas about how he could help, and then he started collecting signatures on a petition to stop the development. He went to public meetings and contacted the newspapers and radio stations in the area about his concern. The development plans were eventually canceled, mainly because this seventh-grader cared enough to fight for animals' homes.[5]

Nine-year-old Roland Tiensuu of Sweden was worried that the rain forests would be gone by the time he grew up. With the help of his teacher, he formed a group called Barnens Regnskog (Children's Rainforest) to raise money to buy rain forests in Costa Rica. In three years, by mid-1991, the group had raised over $1.5 million, and they were able to purchase nearly 3,000 acres. All around the world other children are forming children's rain forest conservation leagues. Roland and his teacher, Eha Kern, were awarded an international Goldman Environmental Prize in 1991 for their efforts.[6]

Volunteer Programs

It takes a lot of time, money, and people to find out the information about animals' habitats and ways of life needed to help them effectively. Scientists who were having trouble getting research funding, found that many people were not only willing to volunteer their time to help but were even willing to pay tuition to get some hands-on experience and learn more about endangered animals and the environment.

Today there are many organizations that use paying volunteers, including EarthWatch and the National Audubon Society. EarthWatch sends out 3,000 volunteers each year to gather research on endangered animals and other environmental problems.[7]

Peter Dutton and Donna McDonald, scientists at the Sea World Research Institute, say that in just five years EarthWatch volunteers helped save more than 33,000 baby sea turtles and helped make the beach site on St. Croix where sea turtles lay their eggs a national wildlife refuge.[8]

Jeanette Jones, a homemaker from Tennessee, is a typical volunteer who wanted to get a little environmental education during her vacation. She wound up crawling on her belly on a Yucatan beach, following a half-ton leatherback sea turtle. It was hard work, but she enjoyed it so much that she spent her next vacation tracking turtles on St. Croix.[9]

Volunteers helping the Caretta Research Project help loggerhead sea turtles in Wassaw Island, Georgia, by searching for turtle nests and helping newly hatched turtles find the water. Turtle-monitoring expeditions in Mexico are sponsored by Foundation for Research, which also offers projects such as helping count sandhill cranes in California. Wildland Studies volunteers can help protect wildlife and preserve wilderness through field studies programs all around the world, ranging from learning about

These birdboxes, made in a classroom in Muncie, Indiana, will provide shelter for songbirds.

whale behavior in Canada to searching for timber wolves in the Northern Cascades.

The January–February 1991 issue of *Buzzworm* lists a directory of environmental education programs for people who want to get involved. For most programs, volunteers must be at least sixteen years old.

Organizations That Help Wildlife Need People's Support

One of the most important ways that people can help endangered animals is to help the groups and organizations that are dedicated to this goal. There are hundreds of organizations concerned with protecting wildlife and wildlife habitats. Most of them depend on financial support from the public. Many schools have special programs, such as aluminum can recycling drives, to raise money to donate to wildlife organizations that save endangered animals.

Many organizations offer special adoption programs. A person who sends a contribution receives an adoption certificate for the animal sponsored. Some programs supply a photograph and background information about the species or a biography of the adopted animal as well.

Adopt-A-Manatee. There are only about 1,500 manatees left in Florida. Since 1974 more than 1,800 have died.[10] Most of the deaths have been caused by humans, including 80 percent due to collisions of watercrafts with the slow-moving, docile water mammals. The Save the Manatee club was formed in 1981 by former Florida

The Save the Manatee Club is helping to protect the manatees in Florida that are threatened by human activities.

governor Bob Graham and singer/songwriter Jimmy Buffett to encourage the public to help save the manatees.

Contributions to the club's Adopt-A-Manatee program are used to help protect and preserve manatees and their habitat. Elementary school classes all around the country have adopted manatees as a class project. Leslie A. McFadden, a teacher in Tennessee, says that her class found it a very rewarding experience. "The children became very interested in protecting not only manatees, but our entire ecosystem."[11]

Adopt-A-Hawk. Steve Hoffman started HawkWatch in 1986 to monitor raptors (predatory birds such as hawks, eagles, falcons, and owls) as they migrate across North America. Each year 30,000 raptors from eighteen species are observed, and about 3,000 are captured, banded, and released so that their progress can be tracked and recorded. Many environmentalists see the health of raptors as an indication of how healthy the entire ecosystem really is. Just as miners used canaries in coal mines as an early warning of poisonous gases, raptors can warn humans about harmful changes in the habitats they feed in.

Through HawkWatch International's Adopt-A-Hawk program, people can adopt raptors. After a *Ranger Rick* article in January 1990, 1,500 children wrote to Hawk-Watch, and 500 children adopted hawks. Students at South Frederick Elementary School in Maryland, for example, set up a "bird bank" in the library and raised enough money to adopt an eagle. They named him "Iron Eagle" and made him the school's official mascot.[12]

Adopt-A-Wolf. Adopt-A-Wolf programs are offered by several groups, such as the Wild Canid Survival and Research Center in Missouri. The center (also known as the Wolf Sanctuary) was founded in 1971 by Marlin Perkins (the host of "Wild Kingdom") and his wife Carol, with the support of others, including Joy and George Adamson, whose story of their experiences with African lions, *Born Free,* helped popularize the plight of endangered animals. Two endangered wolf species, the red wolf and the Mexican wolf, are raised and bred at the sanctuary, which is dedicated to preserving wolves through education and captive breeding. Another adoption program is offered by the Wolf Haven Sanctuary in Washington, which uses the money raised to care for the captive-bred wolves at the sanctuary and to promote wolf conservation.

Both sanctuaries offer tours where students can learn about wolves in the wild. The Wolf Hollow sanctuary of the North American Wolf Foundation in Ipswich, Massachusetts, also permits visitors to see and learn about wolves firsthand. Founded by Paul C. Soffron, Wolf Hollow is the only wolf sanctuary on the east coast.

The Timber Wolf Information Network, which educates teachers, students, and the general public about the recovery of timber wolves in Wisconsin and Michigan, also has an Adopt-A-Wolf program.

Adopt-A-Dolphin. Oceanic Project Dolphin sponsors an Adopt-A-Dolphin program, which helps support studies of dolphins in the wild to determine the best ways of

This red wolf was bred at the Wild Candid Survival and Research Center in Missouri.

protecting them. The project is part of Oceanic Society Expeditions, a nonprofit organization that offers forty-two different expeditions where people can experience many of the wonders of the world, from tropical rain forests and coral reefs to the African plains and highlands.

Adopt-A-Whale. Whales are the largest animals on the earth—even bigger than the dinosaurs were. You can "adopt" a humpback whale through the Whale Adoption Project. A group of fifty whales that spend their summers off the New England coast have been studied and named by scientists at the Center for Coastal Studies in Provincetown, Massachusetts. The project follows and studies the whales each season and monitors their behavior and migration. Foster parents can choose from nearly fifty whales, including Patches, Lightning, Colt, Salt, Pepper, and Cat's Paw. A newsletter keeps foster parents updated on their adopted whale. Adoption programs sponsored by other groups benefit humpback, gray, and right whales.

Learn More About Endangered Animals

Many species that share our world face frightening threats that may ultimately lead to their extinction. But, as we have seen, the picture is not all bleak. Today there are more opportunities than ever before for caring people to help in the fight to save endangered wildlife. Find out more about how you can help from the organizations listed in the "Where to Write" section of this book.

This decal is available from the Whale Adoption Project.

Chapter Notes

Chapter 1

1. Zoological Society of San Diego, "Endangered Species" fact sheet (1989).

2. Patricia West, "Preservation a Piece at a Time," in *Yearbook of Science and the Future 1992* (Chicago: Encyclopaedia Britannica, 1991), pp. 195–209.

3. World Wildlife Fund fact sheet (1991).

4. Jan DeBlieu, "Remodeling the Condor," *The New York Times Magazine* (November 17, 1991), pp. 60–61, 76, 80.

Chapter 2

1. Defenders of Wildlife, "Defending Wildlife" brochure (1991).

2. Defenders of Wildlife, "Saving Endangered Species" (1987 report), pp. 6–7.

3. Ibid.

4. Ken Miller, "Calif. Gray Whales No Longer An Endangered Species," Bridgewater, N.J. *Courier News*, (November 19, 1991), p. A3.

5. Defenders of Wildlife, "Defending Wildlife" brochure (1991).

Chapter 3

1. Laurence Pringle, *Saving Our Wildlife* (Hillside, N.J. Enslow, 1990), p. 16.

2. William Stolzenburg, "Wildlife Connection," *Nature Conservancy* (July/August 1991), pp. 19–25.

3. Ibid.

4. Rainforest Action Network, "Rainforest Action Guide" (undated brochure).

5. Winifred B. Campbell, "Out of the Mouths of Children," *Nature Conservancy* (July/August 1991), p. 7.

6. "Meter-Made Crusade," *Time* (August 12, 1991), p. 59.

7. Walter Corson, ed., *The Global Ecology Handbook* (Boston: Beacon Press, 1990), p. 125.

8. Jon Naar, *Design for a Livable Planet* (New York: Harper, 1990), p. 122.

Chapter 4

1. As quoted in Department of the Interior, U.S. Fish and Wildlife Service, "Endangered Species" (1988 brochure).

2. Defenders of Wildlife, "Saving Endangered Species" (1987 report), p. 18.

3. James Brooke, "Niger Works to Save a Species and Bolster Tribe," *The New York Times* (May 9, 1988), p. A6.

4. "Relief for the Harried Turtle," *Buzzworm: The Environmental Journal* (May/June 1991), p. 12.

5. Lynn Orr Miller, *Endangered Animals* (New York: Beekman House, 1990), pp. 24–25.

6. "Genetic Links May Help Save Rhinos from Extinction," *The New York Times* (October 11, 1989), p. C4.

Chapter 5

1. Patricia West, "Preservation a Piece at a Time," *Yearbook of Science and the Future 1992* (Chicago: Encyclopaedia Britannica 1991), pp. 195–209.

2. Claire Neesham, "All the World's a Zoo," *New Scientist* (August 18, 1990), pp. 31–35.

3. Will Waddell, "The Red Wolf Recovery Project: An Overview," *Wolftracks* (Fall 1991), p. 7.

4. Jane E. Brody, "Making It Safe for Endangered Animals to Go Home Again," *The New York Times* (February 5, 1991), p. C4.

5. Ibid.

6. DeBlieu, Jan, "Remodeling the Condor," *The New York Times Magazine* (November 17, 1991), p. 60–61, 76, 80.

Chapter 6

1. Michael Wallis, "Into the Air, Little Baldies!" *Life* (May 1988), pp. 52–56.

2. Alex Kotlowitz, "All the Right Moves Don't Always Work, Not with Zha-Long," *Wall Street Journal* (October 23, 1991), p. 1.

3. Jan DeBlieu, *Meant To Be Wild*, (Golden, Colo.: Fulcrum, 1991), p. 245.

4. Dirk Johnson, "Tracking the Ferret: A Cooperative Effort Benefits a Former Pest," *The New York Times* (September 24, 1991), p. C4.

Chapter 7

1. Geoffrey Cowley, "Dead Otters, Silent Ducks," *Newsweek*, (April 24, 1989), p. 70.

2. Robert F. Baldwin, "Doctoring the Exotic," *Sea Frontiers* (February 1991), pp. 30–35.

3. Liz Hymans, "To Err is Human: to Clean Wildlife is Divine," *Fifty Plus* (August 1988), p. 18.

4. Doug Lewis, "After an Oil Spill: Saving the Birds," *Sea Frontiers* (July–August 1989), pp. 203–205.

5. Ibid.

6. Associated Press, "Oil Slick Menace," The Newark, N.J. Star Ledger, (July 29, 1991), p. 15.

7. Debbie Ross, "Seven Lucky Birds Free in Neah Bay," *Peninsula Daily News* (August 21, 1991).

8. Thomas Y. Canby, "After the Storm," *National Geographic* (August 1991), pp. 2–32.

9. Claire Neesham, "Out of the Zoo and into the Rainforest," *New Scientist* August 18, 1990), p. 33.

10. Mike Byrne, "Budd Lake Lady Mends Friends on a Wing and a Prayer," The Newark, N.J. *Star Ledger,* (June 13, 1991), p. NW1.

Chapter 8

1. National Wildlife Federation, "You Can Do It!" (1988 booklet).

2. Zoological Society of San Diego, "Endangered Species" fact sheet (1989).

3. Defenders of Wildlife, "Defending Wildlife" brochure (1991).

4. Defenders of Wildlife, "Their Future Is Our Future" brochure (undated).

5. National Wildlife Federation, "You Can Do It!"

6. Elizabeth A. Foley, "Prize Winning Rainforest Protectors," *Dolphin Log* (July 1991), p. 18.

7. Cathy Straight, "Saving Sea Turtles on Vacation," Bridgewater, N.J. *Courier News* (April 22, 1991), p. B6.

8. Ibid.

9. Ibid.

10. Judith Vallee, from a Save the Manatee club fact sheet (November 15, 1991).

11. Nancy Sadusky, Save the Manatee Club fact sheet (undated).

12. Carolyn Marshall-Green, "Iron Eagle," from a HawkWatch International, Inc., fact sheet.

Glossary

artificial insemination—insertion of sperm into the uterus of a female by artificial means (other than normal mating).

biodiversity—the variety of life-forms in a natural community.

captive breeding—breeding and raising animals of endangered species in zoos, refuges, or special breeding centers.

CITES—Convention of International Trade in Endangered Species of Wild Fauna and Flora (an international treaty banning import and export of endangered species).

cloning—production of one or more new organisms from a single body cell.

critical habitat—the land, water, and air that members of an endangered species need for survival, including in their living and breeding places.

double-clutching—removing eggs from nests so birds will lay more.

ecosystem—the interrelated complex of life-forms in a community and their environment.

endangered species—a species in danger of becoming extinct in all or part of its normal habitats.

ESA—Endangered Species Act of 1973, which defined endangered and threatened species and established a cooperative effort to save them.

exotic pets—wild, unusual, or imported animals kept in captivity as companions to humans.

extinct—no longer existing; pertaining to a species of which no living members remain.

habitat—an animal's natural home.

hacking—gradual weaning of captive-bred animals into a wild life.

imprinting—learning to identify with members of the species as a result of exposure to the parents early in life. Recently hatched birds may mistakenly imprint on humans who care for them and later may be unable to mate with their own kind.

in vitro fertilization—the combination of eggs and sperm in a laboratory culture dish. The fertilized eggs are then inserted into the uterus of a female (either the one that produced the eggs or a surrogate mother) to develop into offspring.

migration—seasonal movement of animals from one feeding or breeding area to another.

poaching—hunting or trapping wildlife illegally.

raptors—birds of prey, such as eagles and hawks.

refuge—public or private areas of land set aside for the protection and management of wildlife populations; may also be called preserve, reserve, or sanctuary.

re-introduction—re-population of a natural habitat with captive-bred endangered animals.

species—a group of related animals or plants that can breed with members of their own kind but not (usually) with others.

threatened species—a species that may become endangered if it is not protected.

translocation—moving some members of a species from one place to another.

wildlife corridor—a connection (e.g., a bridge or protected land area) between two habitat areas permitting the safe passage of wildlife.

wildlife rehabilitation—rescue, medical treatment (if needed), and care for injured wildlife designed to restore them to health and return them to their natural habitats or suitable refuges.

Where to Write

African Wildlife Foundation
1717 Massachusetts Ave., NW
Washington, DC 20036
(202) 265-8393

BirdBox Program
Oklahoma Department of
Wildlife Conservation
P.O. Box 53465
Oklahoma City, OK 73152

The Children's Rainforest
P.O. Box 936
Lewiston, ME 04240

The Cousteau Society
930 W. 21st St.
Norfolk, VA 23517
(804) 627-7547

Defenders of Wildlife
1244 19th St., NW
Washington, DC 20036
(202) 659-9510

Desert Fishes Council
P.O. Box 337
Bishop, Ca 93514

EarthWatch
680 Mt. Auburn St.
P.O. Box 403N
Watertown, MA 02272
(617) 926-8200

Environmental Defense
Fund
257 Park Ave.
New York, NY 10010

Foundation for Field
Research
P.O. Box 2010
Alpine, CA 92001
(619) 445-9264

International Crane
Foundation
E-11376 Shady Lane Road
Baraboo, WI 53913
(608) 356-9462

National Aububon Society
950 Third Ave.
New York, NY 10022
(212) 832-3200

National Marine Fisheries
Service
Office of Protective Species
NOAA
Washington, DC 20235
(202) 634-7529

National Wildlife Federation
1412 16th St., NW
Washington, DC 20036
(202) 797-6800

The Nature Conservancy
1815 N. Lynn St.
Arlington, VA 22209
(703) 841-5300

The Peregrine Fund
World Center for
Birds of Prey
5666 W. Flying Hawk Lane
Boise, ID 83709
(208) 362-3716

Project WILD
P.O. Box 18060
Boulder, CO 80308
(303) 444-2390

Rainforest Action Network
301 Broadway, Suite A
San Francisco, CA 94133

Rocky Mountain Raptor
Program
Veterinary Teaching Hospital
300 W. Drake
Fort Collins, CO 80523
(303) 491-0398

Sierra Club
730 Polk St.
San Francisco, CA 94109
(415) 776-2211

Stonehedge Conservatory
31 Elizabeth Lane
Budd Lake, NJ 07828
(201) 691-9275

Sutton Avian Research Center
P.O. Box 2007
Bartlesville, OK 74005

TRAFFIC
1601 Connecticut Ave., NW
Washington, DC 20009

U.S. Fish and Wildlife Service
Publications Unit
Washington, DC 20240

Volunteers for Wildlife
27 Lloyd Harbor Road
Huntington, NY 11743
(516) 423-0982

The Wildlife Society
5410 Grosvenor Lane
Bethesda, MD 20814
(301) 897-9770

World Wildlife Fund
1250 24th St., NW
Washington, DC 20037
(202) 293-4800

The Xerces Society
10 S.W. Ash St.
Portland, OR 97204
(503) 222-2788

Adopt-an-Animal Programs

Adopt-A-Dolphin
Oceanic Society Expeditions
Oceanic Project Dolphin
Fort Mason Center, Building E
San Francisco, CA 94123

Adopt-A-Hawk
HawkWatch International
P.O. Box 35706
Albuquerque, NM 87176
(800) 726-HAWK

Adopt-A-Manatee
Save the Manatee Club
500 N. Maitland
Maitland, FL 32751
(800) 432-JOIN

**Adopt-A-Whale/
Earthtrust**
2500 Pali Hwy.
Honolulu, HI 96817
(808) 595-6927

**Gray Whale Adoption
Program**
The Tarlton Foundation
1160 Battery St., #360
San Francisco, CA 94111

Humpback Adoption Project
International Wildlife
Coalition
634 N. Falmouth Hwy.
P.O. Box 388
North Falmouth, MA
02556-9980

Right Whale Adoption Program
New England Aquarium
Central Wharf
Boston, MA 02110

Adopt-A-Wolf
Timber Wolf Information Network
E110 Emmons Creek Road
Waupaca, WI 54981
(715) 258-7247

Wild Canid Survival and Research Center
P.O. Box 760
Eureka, MO 63025
(314) 938-5900

Wolf Haven International
3111 Offut Lake Road
Tenino, WA 98589
(800) 448-9653

Wolf Hollow
98 Essex St.
Ipswich, MA 01938
(508) 356-0216

Further Reading

Books and Brochures

Caras, Roger. *That Our Children May Know: Vanishing Wildlife in Zoo Portraits.* Stamford, Conn.: Longmeadow Press, 1990.

DeBlieu, Jan. *Meant to Be Wild.* Golden, Colo.: Fulcrum, 1991.

DiSilvestro, Roger L. *The Endangered Kingdom.* New York: Wiley, 1989.

Hendrich, Paula. *Saving America's Birds.* New York: Lothrop, 1982.

Miller, Lynn Orr. *Endangered Animals.* New York: Beekman House, 1990.

Page, Jake. *Zoo: The Modern Ark.* New York: Facts on File, 1990.

Pringle, Laurence. *Saving Our Wildlife.* Hillside, N.J.: Enslow, 1990.

Stretch, Mary Jane. *The Swan in My Bathtub.* New York: Dutton, 1991.

Stuart, Gene S. *Wildlife Alert: The Struggle to Survive.* New York: National Geographic Society, 1980.

U.S. Fish and Wildlife Service. "Why Save Endangered Species?" (brochure)

U.S. Fish and Wildlife Service. "Endangered Species." (brochure) 1988.

Wallace, David Rains. *Life in the Balance.* New York: Harcourt, 1987

West, Patricia. "Preservation a Piece at a Time." In Encyclopaedia Britannica, *Yearbook of Science and the Future 1992.* Chicago: 1991, pp. 195–209.

Wise, William. *Animal Rescue: Saving Our Endangered Wildlife.* New York: Putnam, 1978.

Wildlife Magazines

Audubon Magazine

Buzzworm: The Environmental Journal

National Wildlife

Nature Conservancy

Sea Frontiers

Sierra

Wilderness

Wildlife Conservation

Wings

Index

A addax, 37, 38
Adopt-A-dolphin, 107
Adopt-A-Hawk, 106
Adopt-A-Manatee, 104
Adopt-A-Whale, 109
Adopt-A-Wolf, 107
Adopt-An-Acre, 33
Africa, 27-28, 30, 36
African Wildlife Foundation (AWF), 36–37
Alaska, 79-82
American Forestry Association, 34
Anderson, Esperance, 82
Animal Record Keeping System (Arks), 47
Arhibald, George, 67–68
Artificial insemination, 45
Audubon, John James, 5

B Backyard Wildlife Habitat, 98
bald eagles, 48, 61, 62, 64
The Bald Eagle Protection Act of 1940, 61
Barnens Regnskog, 101
behavior modification, 57–58

Bengal tiger, 28–29, 45
Berkner, Alice, 82-84
bird feeders, 98
Birdbox program, 98, 103
black-footed ferret, 74–77
blue whale, 48
Broley, Charles L., 63
buffalo, 14, 15, 16

C Cade, Tom, 60
California, 82–83
California condor, 48, 54, 55, 56, 57, 58
captive breeding, 44, 54
Caretta Research Project, 102
Chocuyens, 55, 56
CITES (Convention on International Trade in Endangered Species), 19,22
cormorant, 87

D DDT, 60
Defenders of Wildlife, 36
disasters, 79
dolphins, 107
dusky seaside sparrow, 9

E eagles, 48, 61, 62, 64, 84, 106
Earth Watch, 102
embryo bank, 46
endangered species, 17
Endangered Species Act, 54, 70
Endangered Species Act of 1973, 16-17, 35
Endangered and Threatened Wildlife and Plants list, 17
Environmental Protection Agency (EPA), 100
exotic pets, 98, 100
extinction, 6
Exxon Valdez, 79, 82

F falcons, 690, 84, 106
ferrets, 74-77, 76
Foundation for Research, 102

G Galapagos tortoise, 53
Gee Whiz, 67, 68
genetic fingerprints, 47
The George Miksch Sutton Avian Research Center, 63

127

Gila topminnow, 69, 70
gray whales, 19, 109
gray wolf, 36
green sea turtle, 71, 86
greenback cutthroat trout, 19
Grzimek, Bernhard, 30
Grzimek, Michael, 30

H habitat, 8
hand puppets, 55, 64, 65, 66
hawks, 106
hawksbill turtles, 86
"head start" program, 72
heath hen, 10
Hornaday, William, 14
humpback whale, 109, 110
hunting, 7
hurricanes, 87

I in vitro fertilization, 45
inbreeding, 10
Indian desert cat, 45
International Bird Rescue Research Center, 83
International Crane Foundation (ICF), 67, 69
International Union of Conservation of Nature (IUCN), 28

J jaguars, 38
Jakovlev, Peter, 13

K Kelly, Charlene, 93
Kemp's ridley sea turtle, 70
Kenya, 38
koala bears, 8, 48
Kuwait Zoo, 86, 88

L Lindburg, Donald G., 49
lion tailed macaques, 49

M manatees, 104, 105, 106
McBaian, Judith, 80
Mountain Gorilla Project, 38

N National Audubon Society, 102
National Marine Fisheries Service, 17, 42
National Wildlife Federation, 25, 63
The Nature Conservancy, 23, 25, 27, 33, 63

O Oceanic Society Expeditions, 109
oil spill, 40, 79–87
Operation Tiger, 28
owls, 106

P panda, 34
parrots, 87, 100
Patuxent Wildlife Research Center, 63, 65, 69
peregrine falcons, 60, 84
Persian Gulf, 86, 88
pollution, 9, 70

R rabies, 89
radio tracking device, 53, 55
rain forests, 30, 33, 101
raptors, 59
red wolf, 4, 49, 51, 52, 108
refuge, 16, 23, 25, 26
right whales, 109
The Rocky Mountain Raptor Program (RMRP), 91, 92, 93

S salmon, 42
sandhill cranes, 69
Scherpelz, Judy, 91, 93
Sea World Research Institute, 102
Sespe Condor Sanctuary, 55, 56
Sierra Club, 25
Stonehedge Conservatory, 93–95

T threatened species, 17
tigers, 28, 29, 45
timber wolf, 104
translocation of species, 43, 44
turtles, 37, 40, 70, 72, 86

U U.S. Fish and Wildlife Service, 17, 23

V Volunteers for Wildlife, 89, 91

W whales, 19, 88, 104, 109, 110
whooping cranes, 64–68
Wildland Studies, 102
Wolf Compensation Fund, 36
wolves, 4, 36, 49, 51, 104, 107, 108
World Wildlife Fund, 28, 34

X Xerces Society, 59
Xewe, 55

Z zoos, 33, 45–47